T0208411

THE SKETCHING DETECTIVE AND THE SECRET ROBBERY

THE SKETCHING DETECTIVE AND THE SECRET ROBBERY

By

Jack McCormac

Copyright © 2019 by Jack McCormac.

ISBN: Softcover   978-1-7960-5627-3
             eBook   978-1-7960-5626-6

All rights reserved. No part of this book may be reproduced or transmitted in any form or by any means, electronic or mechanical, including photocopying, recording, or by any information storage and retrieval system, without permission in writing from the copyright owner.

This is a work of fiction. Names, characters, places and incidents either are the product of the author's imagination or are used fictitiously, and any resemblance to any actual persons, living or dead, events, or locales is entirely coincidental.

Any people depicted in stock imagery provided by Getty Images are models, and such images are being used for illustrative purposes only. Certain stock imagery © Getty Images.

Print information available on the last page.

Rev. date: 09/06/2019

To order additional copies of this book, contact:
Xlibris
1-888-795-4274
www.Xlibris.com
Orders@Xlibris.com
802071

Contents

This book is dedicated to the people who have kept Edisto Beach non-commercialized and family oriented.

Chapter One

Sea Fever

My name is Jack MacKay. I am an Assistant Professor of Civil Engineering at the university in our home town. My lovely architect wife Fiona (with her fiery red hair and temperament) and I decided to take a several week summer vacation at Edisto Beach, a part of the subtropical Edisto Island, South Carolina. The beach is family oriented with a several mile long sand beach, several hundred homes, a pavilion, a few stores and restaurants, a golf course and a state park with a campground. It is one of the few non-commercialized beaches still existing in the United States. There are no high rise hotels, no large businesses, and condominiums are at a minimum. To find a red light you have to drive your car for over twenty miles back on the highway that comes to the beach.

Edisto Island is a fairly large island about twelve miles long and twelve miles wide. It is bounded by the North and South Edisto Rivers, the Dawhoo River, the Intracoastal Waterway, and the Atlantic Ocean. It is one of the barrier islands of the South Carolina coast and is made up of a rather large number of smaller islands. This fact is quite evident if you fly over the island when the tide is high. At high tide the numerous large tidal creeks, in effect, cut the main island up into numerous separate pieces such as the islands named Botany Bay, Pockoy, Eddingsville (the ill-fated), Little Edisto, Edisto Beach, Whooping and others. Supposedly the residents of Whooping Island long ago would whoop for the ferry to come get them when they wished to travel elsewhere.

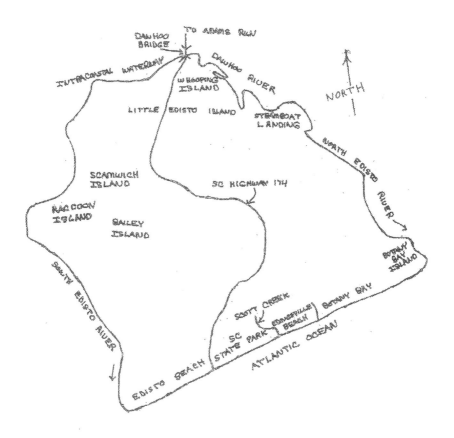

Edisto Island, South Carolina

Edisto Island Map

Edisto Island was originally settled by an Indian tribe called the Edistows (one of several spellings). The Edistows apparently lived there peacefully for many centuries. In the 1500s the Spanish discovered the island and named it Oristo, which some people say means gold in Spanish. The name Oristo may have just been another name for the local Indian tribes. (Oristo was the name originally given to the island golf course, but it is now named the Plantation Course at Edisto.) Unfortunately, the Europeans brought sickness to the natives. By the early 1700s most of the Edistows had been wiped out by smallpox and it, together with other illnesses, killed the rest of them soon after.

The English followed the Spanish in the 1600s. It is said the Earl of Shaftsbury, one of the original eight Lords Proprietors, purchased Edisto Island in 1674 from the Edistows with some beads, cloth, hatchets, and other goods. The English who began to raise indigo and rice on the island are the ones who first brought black slaves to Edisto. As it turned out, raising rice was not altogether successful because of the high salinity of the many marshes in the area and the lack of freshwater ponds that hindered rice planting and growing. On the other hand, the raising of indigo was extremely successful.

Indigo dye is a compound with a distinct blue color similar to that used today in blue jeans. In those days a significant part of the world's supply of indigo dye was produced from plants grown on Edisto Island. As blue dyes were so rare in the world, the Edisto crops brought immense wealth to its planters. However, the main market was Great Britain. After the American Revolution that market dried up, and the planters switched to growing long staple cotton. The fibers of this cotton are much longer than those of the usual upland cotton and are also appreciably stronger. This cotton raised at Edisto, known as "Sea Island Cotton," was one of the finest cottons ever grown in the world and brought unbelievable wealth to the island. This cotton was so revered around the world that the Vatican at one time insisted the Pope's clothes be made from it.

The cotton industry flourished and magnificent plantations with historic mansions were built. Today twenty-nine plantations, homes, and churches on the island are listed in the National Registry of Historic Places. The names of the great homes and plantations on Edisto are very realistic and descriptive. Some examples are Blue House, Old Home, Ocean View, Rabbit Point, Salt Landing, Green Point, Shell House (foundations built of tabby, an old type of coastal concrete formed by mixing equal parts of lime, water, sand, oyster shells, and ash.), Bay View, Gun Bluff, Botany Bay (an area notorious in colonial days as a pirate rendezvous), and others.

Farming Sea Island cotton continued unabated until the War of Northern Aggression (also known as the Civil War, the War Between the States, or The Late Great Unpleasantness). During the war the great plantations were effectively destroyed. However, after the war cotton farming was resumed and enormous wealth was again achieved. As the years went by, however, the boll weevils began to destroy the cotton crops and pretty well finished them off by the 1920s. The islanders then switched to truck gardening, cattle raising and shrimping. The shrimp industry was so successful at one time that several dozen shrimp trawlers worked the nearby waters. Unfortunately, in recent years that business has been greatly reduced because of the foreign shrimp farms and today there are only a few active trawlers.

After the Revolutionary War many families, wealthy from the great cotton plantations, built a resort village on an island just north of Edisto Beach. Known as Eddingsville, it was connected to the main island by a causeway built from sea shells and black marsh mud. These families would move to Eddingsville early in the summer and stay there until the fall. Apparently the delightful sea breezes greatly reduced the presence of mosquitoes and the consequent malaria. Unfortunately, the island was substantially wiped away by a severe hurricane in 1893.

Until a wooden bridge was built to Edisto in about 1920 across what is now the Intracoastal Waterway, visitors had to come by boat or travel at low tide over a sort of causeway built with mud and oyster shells to gain access. After the bridge was built many people began to vacation at Edisto Beach. They built rather crude summer homes, at least as compared to the expensive homes of today. However, a very large percentage of these modest homes were destroyed by a hurricane in 1940. Since that time the beach area has been rebuilt and greatly expanded. Many of the homes built in the last few decades are very large and expensive, some almost rivaling the great plantation homes of the past.

The earlier wood frame houses seem to have been open and friendly to other vacationers. I doubt that their owners were overly concerned when people tracked in sand or sat on their furniture in wet bathing suits. Today you would have a hard time getting by with such behavior in the carpeted and air conditioned homes that are so commonplace at Edisto. I sometimes wonder if today's visitors enjoy the beach as much as those visitors of a few decades ago in their less pretentious but more open and friendly homes.

Edisto Beach is an incorporated town with zoning laws that have successively kept away the large modern structures common to the more urban beaches. These laws that limit buildings to a maximum of four living units per acre and to maximum heights of forty feet (chimneys can extend to greater heights) have limited the construction of motels, hotels and condominiums. Furthermore, the city does not have a central sewage treatment plant. This fact along with the minimum acreage requirement effectively prevents the development of large commercial enterprises.

During our preparations for going to Edisto I said to Fiona, "I need to warn you in advance about the city water on the island. It is treated and safe to drink, but it sure doesn't taste like it. Some of my friends say it has body. Whatever it contains, the water reminds me of rotten eggs."

Fiona frowned. "Well, I'm telling you, that sounds totally disgusting! Maybe I should just take my own water, and you can drink the water with body."

My explanation continued, "Many of the newer and more expensive homes on the island, not including the one we've rented, have reverse osmosis equipment for taking away the awful taste. With reverse osmosis the water is moved through semi-permeable membranes. The water goes through but not salts, dyes, bacteria, and other impurities. The result is good drinking water. We poorer peons without the availability of reverse osmosis have three choices:

1.   We can just hold our noses and try to drink the city water.
2.   We can purchase bottled water.

3. We can drive to the town fire station where they have reverse osmosis and good tasting water that the town provides free of charge to everyone."

Fiona's frown persisted. "Well, thank you for an engineer's perspective on water systems. Knowing you as I do, it doesn't surprise me that you chose the cheaper house without the reverse osmosis. We wouldn't want to spend an extra penny on good tasting water, would we? Well, I won't be the one driving to the fire station!"

I overlooked her comments and continued. "Some of your friends who are addicted to drinking endless cups of coffee or tea each day could easily break the habit by coming to Edisto and preparing their beverages with city water. I think after they drank two or three cups prepared this way they would never again want a cup of coffee or tea prepared in any way."

Fiona simply shook her head, rolled her eyes, and walked away.

When asked whether they enjoy their trips to Edisto, many South Carolinians reply, "No. It's an awful place. You wouldn't like it." They, however, seem to keep going there at frequent intervals. What they are really saying is, "We want to keep this place just like it is forever. We don't want it overrun with tourists, traffic, motels, and neon signs." Perhaps this constancy of the island year after year adds to its attractiveness.

If you were to ask me what I thought of Edisto, I would say, "What a dreadful place to go on a vacation! It has gnats, mosquitoes, horseflies and no-seeums. The drinking water smells and tastes like rotten eggs and will turn your stomach upside down. The place has almost no stores or shops, only a few small restaurants, no circus rides, and the people are so friendly that you don't have any privacy. By the way, I can't wait until I get back."

As Fiona and I drove toward the coast we stopped for lunch in the town of Orangeburg, South Carolina. While we waited for the nice waitress to bring our lunches, Fiona questioned me. "So this is Orangeburg. Do they grow oranges in South Carolina? I certainly have not seen any orange groves around here. Where in the world did they get the name 'Orangeburg'?"

As a long-winded professor, I just love to explain or, as Fiona says, lecture. "The name of the town was not adopted because of the presence of orange groves as there are none. Rather it was named for the Englishman William IV, Prince of Orange. The Orange Order, originally the Orange Society, was an Irish protestant and political society."

Fiona smiled, "I do learn so much from your lectures."

As we came out of the restaurant located near an elementary school, we could hear a class of young children enthusiastically belting out the song "Sandlappers" written by Mrs. Nelle McMaster Sprott of Winnsboro, South Carolina.

We are good Sandlappers
Yes, we're good Sandlappers
And we're mighty proud to say
That we live
Yes, we live
In the very best state
Of the USA.

Fiona was impressed. "Listen to those beautiful children singing that wonderful song. But, risking another lecture, I must ask. What in the world is a Sandlapper?"

The professor in me got another chance! "Well, Fiona, the nickname 'Sandlappers' is frequently used for South Carolinians. The true origin of this word is not really known, but there are several theories as to why the term is used. Millions of years ago the ocean covered the lower half of the present state. As a result, much of the area extending for over 100 miles from the present coast is quite sandy. Because of this fact, I have always thought the reason for the term was that the sand lapped over a good deal of the state."

"That makes some sense, I guess. Now I can add 'Sandlapper' to my list of nicknames for you!"

"Thank you very much. I'm very proud of that name," I responded.

I did not share with Fiona that there are several other more prevalent theories used to explain the name. Perhaps the theory most accepted is the one concerning the practice of eating dirt by some of the early residents. Apparently some of the poorer people in the state would eat, along with their meals, a spoon or two of dirt. Some present day researchers claim the practice of dirt eating may well have been for the purpose of providing iron and some other minerals to the diet perhaps equivalent to vitamin pills today. Many other minerals the human body needs are also contained in dirt. Some people today believe the eating of dirt can make them look more attractive. They say the practice improves the color of their skin and softens it. (It hasn't helped my skin at all.) By the way, the civil engineering professors in my foundation classes insisted we call it soil and not dirt.

When I get within twenty miles of the ocean, there seems to be something in the air that quickens my breath and exhilarates me. This was the situation when we arrived at Adams Run, a village about eighteen miles inland from Edisto Beach. With that feeling I began to recite John Masefield's wonderful poem "Sea Fever."

I must down to the seas again, to the lonely sea and the sky,
And all I ask is a tall ship and a star to steer her by,
And the wheel's kick and the wind's song and the white sail's shaking,
And a grey mist on the sea's face and a grey dawn breaking.

I must down to the seas again, for the call of the running tide
Is a wild call and a clear call that may not be denied;
And all I ask is a windy day with the white clouds flying,
And the flung spray and the blown spume, and the seagulls crying.

I must down to the seas again to the vagrant gypsy life.
To the gull's way and the whale's way where the wind's like a whetted knife;
And all I ask is a merry yarn from a laughing fellow-rover,
And quiet sleep and a sweet dream when the long trick's over.

On the way from Adams Run to Edisto Beach you may very well begin to fall in love with this area. I hoped Fiona would also love it. As we drove she commented in amazement, "Look at this. Both sides of the highway for long stretches are lined with trees. It must look very different in the winter when they don't have any leaves. What kind of trees are these?"

"They are called live oaks because they are evergreens. In March they do shed some leaves as new leaf buds edge the old leaves from their stems. These magnificent always green trees rarely grow to heights more than forty to sixty feet, but their unbelievable limbs may extend outwards for distances greater than the tree heights. Not far to the north of Edisto there is on John's Island an exceptionally large and famous live oak tree. This 1400 or 1500 year old tree, named "Angel Oak," is sixty-five feet high. One of its limbs has a circumference of seventeen feet and extends outward for eighty-nine feet."

"Astonishing!" an astounded Fiona mutters. "We must visit Angel Oak one day."

The limbs on live oaks often come together over roads creating lovely canopies or tunnels just like the road we were traveling on. Hanging from the limbs is the handsome, silvery Spanish moss, sometimes called "old man's beard." Native Americans referred to the moss as being "tree hair" while French explorers trying to insult their Spanish exploring rivals called it "Spanish beard." It later became known as "Spanish moss." It grows on cypress and gum trees as well as on live oaks but seems to slip off pines and palms. Many people think the moss will kill its host trees, but this is not correct as it is not a parasite. It takes nothing from the trees and lives only on moisture and minerals from the air and sunlight. Thus it is an air plant (called an epiphyte).

Supposedly, Henry Ford stuffed the seats in his first Model T's with Spanish moss. Some people use the moss to make tea they say helps relieve rheumatism, birth pains, toothaches, and so on. Many birds and animals use it for bedding in their nests. I hate to think of any of them, human or otherwise, taking that lovely moss from the trees.

The last approximate fifteen miles of the trip involve crossing quite a few salt marshes. Fiona exclaimed, "Look at this view. It is entirely different from that tunnel made by the oak trees. Now all I can see is this flat, flat land with grasses but no trees."

My lecture on the coastal country continued. "These are transitional areas between the land and the ocean. South Carolina has the largest area of salt marshes of any of the Atlantic coast states. About one-seventh of the marshes in South Carolina were caused by man-made impoundments developed for the rice fields before the 'Late Great Unpleasantness.' After the war, rice farms, once so common in the South Carolina coastal area, were no longer competitive economically because of the lack of cheap slave labor.

"There are incredibly large numbers of shrimp, crabs, and fish that use the marshes as their nursery where there is much food and some protection from their predators. Sadly, about fifty percent of the salt marshes in the United States have been destroyed. A large part of this destruction occurred between about 1950 and 1978. During those years we filled and drained a great deal of the marshes for the purpose of developing more places for homes, industry, and agriculture near the sea. It was not uncommon to have new beach lots created by pumping sand into the marshes from river beds and the ocean bottom. I would think these rather unstable lots will be the first things to go in the event of a strong hurricane. Further damage to the marshes was caused by the innumerable drainage ditches dug for the control of mosquitoes."

Enjoying the view, Fiona mused, "That marsh grass looks like a wheat field or the waving grass prairies of our western United States."

I had to smile at her thoughts. "Yes, it does. Put your window down and enjoy the smell of the sea. As the tide comes in it covers the marshes almost to the top of the grass. During the falling tide the marshes are drained down to mud flats. I have read that the amount of organic material created on very fine inland farms can run from roughly two to four tons per acre per year. Supposedly salt marshes are so rich and productive they can produce from five to about nine or ten tons of organic material per acre per year.

"From this brief description you can see why various state laws have been enacted to protect the marshes. These marshes are the very foundation of countless species of plankton and invertebrates.

"The marshes trap sediment running off the nearby islands as well as the mainland. The decay of leaves and stems of the marsh growth further help build up the peaty soil of the marsh. This semi-liquid soil is called muck or pluff mud. Each incoming tide floods the marsh grass and stirs up the rich nutrients in the mud. This provides food for the various plankton, fish, and shellfish to live on. When the tide goes out, the marshes seem to come alive with the visits of birds, raccoons, and deer looking for fish, bugs, snails, crabs, and other things to eat."

Fiona responded with her typical attitude, "Listen to you. This isn't even engineering stuff, but I can count on you to know all about it. I think you must really like this place."

I took a deep breath of sea air and smiled.

Finally the highway crosses a rather short causeway through the marsh and onto the beach area. It is my very strong opinion that the Edisto Beach town officials should place the following sign at the point where you come off the causeway:

WARNING
DANGER

THE UNITED STATES GOVERNMENT WARNS
PEOPLE VISITING THIS AREA OF THE DANGER
OF THEFT. THIS ISLAND MAY VERY WELL
STEAL YOUR HEART.

Chapter Two

Beach Activities

iona and I had rented a house on the main drag at Edisto Beach. This street, Palmetto Boulevard, runs parallel and close to the edge of the ocean. Our house was located on the ocean side of the road where many of the houses, due to beach erosion, are almost in the water at spring tides. Spring tides are the highest tides that occur at or slightly after new moons and full moons.

During the last few weeks before we made this trip we started saving our plastic milk jugs. As soon as we had taken our possessions into the house, I took the jugs and drove to the fire department to obtain some of the good tasting water. Upon returning to the house Fiona and I had a brief swim and then got down to the serious business of visiting this beach—that is searching for fossils. Edisto is famed for the fossils that have been found on its shores. The most common items are sharks' teeth. Only a few decades ago they were extremely numerous at Edisto along with many other fossils. These included teeth and bones from all sorts of creatures that once lived here on the land or in the sea or both. There were bison, whales, alligators, giant beavers, camels, giant armadillos, tapirs, rhinoceroses, and others. In addition to these creatures there were elk and deer and visits by the great loggerhead turtles.

Most of the fossils found on the island are from the Pleistocene epoch. This was the period running from about 2.6 million years ago until about twelve thousand years ago. During the Pleistocene epoch there were repeated glaciations of the earth. A few of the fossils found at Edisto, such as bones and teeth from the three toed horse, are said to be from a time before the Pleistocene epoch. I made sketches of some of the fossils we have found on our trips to the island.

HAMMERHEAD SHARK'S TOOTH.

SPINAL DISK OF A SHARK

TOOTH FROM A 3 TOED SMALL HORSE

ALLIGATOR TOOTH

CAMEL'S TEETH

Some fossils we have fo at Edisto Beach

Fossils

During the past several decades so much publicity has been put out by various real estate and tourist agencies concerning the fossils found at Edisto that thousands of fossil hunters have descended on the island from all over the country and even foreign countries, particularly Canada. As a result, good fossil finds are few and far between at Edisto today.

Despite this great decrease of available fossils, a person first coming to this beach might very well think that most of the people here are physically deformed due to back or neck problems. As you walk along the beach it sometimes seems that everyone you see is bent over looking down at the sand in front of their feet or crawling along among the shells. These positions are referred to as the "Edisto Crouch."

Variations of the Edisto Crouch

Edisto Crouch

In addition to the previously mentioned fossils there are many other items found on the Edisto shore such as conch shells, starfish, and sand dollars (formerly called sea biscuits by South Carolina children).

I said to Fiona in my college professor voice, "The sand dollar is also frequently referred to as the Holy Ghost Shell because many people say its markings represent the birth, crucifixion, and resurrection of Jesus. You can easily see the Easter lily on each shell and at the center of the lily is the star that led the shepherds and the wise men to the place of Jesus' birth. The five slots around the shell represent the four nail holes and the spear wound to the body of Jesus caused by the Roman soldiers. Should you break open a sand dollar you will find five little white shells that represent five doves waiting to spread goodwill and grace to the world. This legend serves to remind us of our hope for the resurrection and a new life.

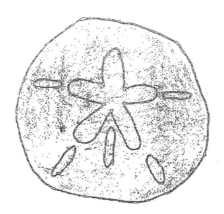

A sand dollar (usually two to four inches in diameter)

Sand Dollar

"The true name of the southern sand dollar is the keyhole urchin, a name given to it by the five evenly spaced keyholes or slots. In other parts of the world there are sand dollars with no slots or with a different number of them."

Fiona pulled a sand dollar out of her collection bag and examined it, fingering the things I had described. "This one I have is white but the one you are holding is brownish. Are they the same?"

"Many of the sand dollars found on the beach have been bleached white by the sun like the one you have. These are dead and probably OK to put in your house. On the other hand, you will often find rather dark brown sand dollars in the edge of the water or near it. These are either still alive or only recently deceased. You don't want to take these into your home because within a few days they will smell to high heaven. If you want to keep them you probably should soak them for a number of hours in vinegar and then put them outside for several days until the sun bleaches them white. Only then should you provide them with inside residence."

Soon after we started walking along the beach I picked up a lovely, shiny shell about three inches long and said, "Fiona, this is the official South Carolina state shell, the olive. As children we used to call them bullets or rockets because of their shape. I understand the Indians loved them as we do and used them as beads."

The South Carolina state shell, the olive (two to three inches long)

Olive

Again Fiona reached into her bag. "Look, the olive I found is larger than the one you have. Maybe I will start a collection of olives."

I mentioned the tremendous number of shark's teeth that have been found on Edisto Beach through the years. They are usually black due to fossilization. Most of the ones found on the beach are between one half and two inches long. Yet I'm sure you have seen giant shark's teeth from six to eight inches long for sale in beach shops along the coast. These teeth, often from extinct prehistoric monstrous sharks, are seldom found along the beaches today. They are usually found by divers swimming along the bottoms of various water bodies along the coast. In South Carolina the coastal waters are murky with fine sediment. As a consequence, the divers cannot see in the dark deep waters even with lights. Therefore, they swim along on the bottom of rivers, bays, and the ocean feeling with their hands. Though they may find some great things, this practice does not appeal to me. I'm not sure what I might find or what might find me.

After supper we decided to go to the state park to the north of the beach to listen to one of the loggerhead turtle lectures given on certain nights in the summer. A park ranger presented an excellent talk on these sea creatures to a fascinated and enthusiastic group of people. I have tried to present his words verbatim.

"Some of the great loggerhead turtles come in to Edisto to lay their eggs each year between mid-May and August. They are an endangered species for several reasons. The greatest threats to their continued existence are the unintentional and intentional acts of humans. They may be unintentionally captured by men with their nets, traps, pots, fishing lines, and dredges. In the Bahamas, Cuba, and Mexico they are intentionally harvested for food purposes.

"These giant turtles, named loggerheads because of their large log shaped heads, live to be fifty or more years of age. Their shells can be as much as four feet long, and they can weigh up to five hundred pounds. If you have ever been stung by a jellyfish, you will probably be very pleased to know that jellyfish make up a significant part of the diet of these turtles.

"Loggerheads do not usually reach sexual maturity until they are about twenty-five or thirty years old. The mature females lay an average of about 110 or 120 eggs once every two or three years. The eggs look a little like ping pong balls and are about the same size. The mother crawls up on the beach, digs a hole with her flippers, lays her eggs, covers them up with sand, and heads back to the ocean. The eggs hatch in about fifty-three to fifty-eight days in South Carolina. Then the young turtles struggle up out of the sand and head to the ocean."

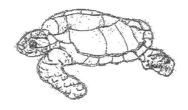

The loggerhead turtle (May be up to four feet long
and weigh up to five hundred pounds)

Loggerhead Turtle

After the ranger finished speaking, I began to spout off to Fiona my limited knowledge of these giant turtles. "Loggerheads live a rough life, particularly when they are young. It is believed that only one in a thousand or maybe not more than one in ten thousand survive to adulthood. The math doesn't work out well for turtles. The average female turtle lays in her lifetime about 4 times 110 or 120 eggs=440 or 480. Each of those eggs has a 1/1000 or less chance of survival. I haven't even considered that say only about one half of the surviving turtles are female. The net result of this stunning math is that each female turtle has well less than an even chance of producing a single turtle that will reach adulthood. No wonder loggerheads are an endangered species.

"The eggs and the baby turtles are gobbled up by all sorts of predators on the beach and in the ocean. The females who survive will usually return to the area where they were born to lay their eggs twenty-five or thirty years later. They seem to lay them at night. I guess there is much less danger from predators during those times. You can stand right by a turtle as she lays her eggs and she will appear to be oblivious of your presence. During the egg laying process she seems to be shedding tears sometimes. I'm sure I would shed a bushel of tears if I had to lay over 100 ping pong ball sized eggs.

"During the egg-laying months various groups, usually consisting of volunteers, search the beaches early in the morning to see if any of the turtles have crawled in to lay their eggs. Their crawling trails are quite easy to see—that is, until the next tide washes them away. If a turtle has come in, a volunteer checks the location of the eggs. If it is felt the nest is too close to the ocean, where the eggs might be uncovered and washed away by the tides, the volunteer will carefully dig up and move the eggs to higher ground.

"In any case, a wire screen is placed over the nests to protect them from predators. Raccoons who flourish on the South Carolina coastal islands are very fond of these eggs. There are also some two-legged mammals that also love to have the eggs as part of their diet. You might think the volunteers would shoot the raccoons as they gather around the nests, and I'm sure they would like to. However, it doesn't seem quite right for them to protect the endangered turtle species while at the same time they try to kill off another species although that species is not endangered. As a result, the raccoons are flourishing. The volunteers put up notices on posts by the turtle nests indicating the presence of the eggs. They record the dates when the eggs were laid thus people will know the approximate dates when the eggs will hatch."

Shortly after the ranger finished his talk he took us on a beach walk to a few of the fifty-three to fifty-eight day old turtle nests to try to see the baby turtles hatching. At the second nest the little turtles were coming up out of the sand. As a matter of fact, we counted nearly a hundred of them. It was surely a wonderful and exciting experience for us. The hatchlings are about 1 ¾ inches long, ¾ of an inch wide, and they each weigh about ¾ of an ounce. They range in color from light brown to almost black. They hatch mostly during the night when the darkness lessens their chances of being gobbled up by birds, animals, or humans. Also the sand at night is not as hot as in the daytime when they might be injured by the heat.

Baby sea turtles are attracted by light. Under natural conditions the ocean water is the brightest thing they will see. The water is lighted by the reflection from the moon and stars. As a result, they crawl toward the sea. However, if streetlights or houselights are visible from the beach, the turtles may very well mistakenly head for them crawling onto streets and exposing themselves to cars and other dangers including predators. Thus, you can see why the South Carolina beaches have laws which prohibit the presence of outside lights shining toward the beaches.

As a result of the hazards mentioned, the volunteers, working to preserve the turtles, will try to herd the baby turtles safely to the ocean. I understand that these workers are instructed not to carry the babies to the water. Supposedly if they crawl on their own to the ocean, the females will return to the same beach twenty-five or so years later to lay their own eggs. If they are carried to the water, they make no biological imprint of the beach thus cannot return to the same location when it is time to lay their eggs. (Anyway, this is what the turtle experts say.)

Chapter Three

A Bombshell in Charleston

Two days after we arrived at Edisto, Fiona and I were reading the Charleston newspaper, *The Post and Courier*. On the front page there was an astounding story concerning a robbery and murder that had occurred the year before. The writer of the article retold the story of the crimes as to how a lone, masked male gunman had robbed the First Universe Bank on Meeting Street one morning and during the process had shot and killed an uncooperative bank teller.

The writer went on to say that a week before, an Army veteran from Upstate South Carolina named Robert Musgrove died at the Veterans Hospital in Columbia. However, before he died he confessed that he, the year before, had robbed the First Universe Bank in Charleston and shot a bank teller.

After a stenographer was rushed into his room he repeated his confession, and she recorded his exact words. When asked if anyone else was involved in the crime he replied, "No. I did it alone and got all the money myself. As soon as I got the money I walked outside, got into my car and drove out of Charleston never to return." Here he laughed weakly and said, "I have always heard that robbers frequently return to the scene of their crimes and get arrested. I didn't want that to happen to me so I left town for good."

Later when a copy of his confession was transmitted to the Charleston police, they studied it in great detail and concluded that Mr. Musgrove was the perpetrator of those crimes. They said the details of his confession checked out in every way but one and that concerned the amount of money taken. This discrepancy was like the explosion of a bombshell, and it shook the city almost as much as the 1886 earthquake.

Mr. Musgrove said he had earned $110,000 for just a few minutes work at the bank. He further said he had spent almost all of it and was planning to withdraw money from a bank in the Five Points area of Columbia just as he had done earlier in Charleston. It was his intent to move on to Myrtle Beach after his planned Columbia banking activity. Unfortunately, before he could carry out his new plan, he became ill and was admitted to the hospital with incurable cancer. The astounding thing about his statement was the fact that the bank had claimed $600,000 was missing and not $110,000. One of the witnesses to the confession at the hospital said she remembered reading a newspaper story concerning the robbery where it said the bank had lost $600,000 not $110,000. Therefore, she asked Mr. Musgrove if he had counted the money. He replied, "I had never seen such a pile of money before so I counted it three times. It was $110,000."

Mr. Musgrove further said he had read the $600,000 figure in the paper himself and just thought the bank was trying to rook the insurance people. That didn't worry him at all as he thought those people had plenty of money and wouldn't miss a few hundred thousand dollars here or there. As he was on his deathbed, there seemed to be no reason to doubt his word. Shortly after the robbery, the bank auditors had confirmed that the bank was short the larger amount, and the insurance company lived up to its commitment and paid the money.

As a result of this confession, the city of Charleston suddenly seemed to be filled with a whirlwind of gossip. This was true for *The Post and Courier* and the local radio and televisions stations. When local persons were overheard at their conversations a listener would frequently hear the words "that crooked bank." The city was swamped with rumors to the effect that one or more of the bank officials had absconded with the extra $490,000. People would say, "They pay almost no interest on our deposits, probably because they steal any money that could be used for that purpose."

The net result of all this was near disaster for the bank. A large number of the bank's depositors decided bank employees might run off with their deposits. Apparently they didn't have faith in the federal government's guarantees for such deposits, and they began to move their money to other banks or even to private hiding places. There was almost a run on the bank.

The two of us sat in our rented beach house thinking of the newspaper article and posing questions about the affair that neither one of us could answer. Picture the situation. An armed man entered the bank, shot a teller and escaped with a large sum of money. The police were immediately called and arrived within a few minutes. From that moment forward the bank was a busy place with bank employees and quite a few policemen rubbing elbows with each other.

Was it possible during this time for another robber to sneak in and conduct an even larger theft than the first one and not be seen? That didn't seem to be possible to either one of us. Fiona asked, "How could anyone in broad daylight rob the bank in front of all those people and get away with it?"

I responded, "The more we talk about this situation the more I get the feeling the two robberies are related in some way. What are the odds of this bank being robbed twice on the same day, apparently after having been located here for many years without a single incident of this type occurring?

"It seems to me as though the second robber knew there was going to be a first robber or at least was prepared to immediately act if there was a robbery. By this I mean that I have the feeling the second robbery would not have occurred unless there was a first one. Furthermore, the second robbery was so smooth that its perpetrator correctly thought any money taken would be credited to the first robber."

Fiona exclaimed, "Romeo, for once in a blue moon or two you may have hit the nail on the head with your ideas! In some way someone secretly took a big pile of money and no one realized it happened. In effect, the second robber planned to rob the bank only if someone else robbed the bank first."

I responded, "All of what we have said points in one direction and that is to an insider who is associated with the bank. Also the second robber must have planned his robbery long in advance for it to have gone so smoothly. Except for the death bed confession of Mr. Musgrove it might never have been discovered and all the missing money would have been credited to him for always."

As Fiona thought about this that certain look came over her face. I know that look well. "There are so many questions we can't answer. How could the second robber take the money without being observed? It seems impossible that he could walk around the bank stuffing stacks of bills in a satchel. Also, how could he get the money out of the bank after he took it? What did he do with the money after he took it out of the bank?

"I'm sure there is going to be considerable criticism of the police for allowing a second robbery to take place right under their noses. Admittedly they had no way of knowing they were dealing with two robberies instead of just one. In fact, it was almost a year later that the second robbery was accidentally discovered when Mr. Musgrove confessed. All they knew was the robber arrived, shot a teller, left the bank, and then vanished with a considerable sum of money in his possession. They had no idea that a second robbery had occurred, thus they were not thinking of additional ways money could be taken and removed from the bank. Nevertheless, I think the newspapers will jump all over the police."

As I should have expected, Fiona began to moan, "Why can't we get involved in this bank investigation?" If there is any mystery anywhere around within one thousand miles or more, she wants to be right in the middle of it, and the worse the crime the better she likes it. I admit that I don't really mind, but please don't tell her.

I responded to her question, "We are supposedly here on vacation, and we don't need to be mixed up in the situation. The Charleston police are far more competent to handle the investigation than we are."

On the day after the news of the confession and death of Mr. Musgrove was reported, *The Post and Courier* printed a scathing editorial concerning the efficiency of the Charleston Police Department. The officers were described as being fat, lazy, rude, incompetent, and overpaid. Reference was made to the fact that they investigated and investigated for a year the first robbery and murder at the First Universe Bank with no results whatsoever other than a considerable expenditure of taxpayers' money.

"Then by luck the villain confessed his crimes on his deathbed," said the editorial writer. He went on to say that Mr. Musgrove's confession was not in any way due to the work of the noble Charleston officers. Nevertheless, he assumed the department would claim full credit for solving another crime.

The editorialist, a Mr. Guignard (pronounced GHIN-yard), continued sarcastically saying that he hoped the second robber was very old and in exceedingly poor health. He expressed the hope that the life of the man who was the second robber of the bank was coming to an end in the near future, and he would make a full deathbed confession of his crimes. In that way investigators would be able to claim they had racked up another criminal. (My thoughts to all of this were, "If you think it's so easy to catch a clever robber like this one, why don't you get out and do it yourself?")

Chapter Four

The Holy City

One morning Fiona and I were sitting in the rocking chairs on the front porch of our rental house looking out over the ocean. I said to her, "Fiona, you and I have been planning to visit Charleston a few times during our stay here at the beach. Since you have never been there, I've been thinking I should tell you a few of the things I have learned about the city during my lifetime. Perhaps this will make your visits more enjoyable and maybe you will understand a little why I, and so many others, have such a love for the place."

Fiona responded, "OK. I'm ready for the lecture. Should I take notes? Will there be a test?"

Trying to ignore her comments, I continued, "As you know, I went to college there for four years and during that time always thought Charleston was one great place. It was originally named Charles Towne in 1670 when it was founded. In 1783, however, the name was changed to Charleston. Today many people refer to it as the Holy City for at least two reasons. First, if you look at the skyline of the city from a distance you will see that it is dotted with numerous lovely church steeples. One thing that makes the steeples stand out so prominently is the absence of other tall buildings because of strict city building code restrictions on heights for both commercial and residential projects. A second reason is from its first days Charleston has been one of the most religiously tolerant cities in America. In its early days the people welcomed Protestants, Jews, Huguenots and many other religious groups. I must admit, however, that Catholics were not usually on the list of those welcomed. Many of the original people moving to the city had come to America to escape persecution by the Catholic Church in Europe. As a result, they didn't think too highly of Catholics. Today the city continues to be quite tolerant of all sorts of religious groups, and Catholics seem to me now to have made the list."

Fiona chimed in, "I recently read that the Conde' Nast Traveler, one of the premier travel magazines in the world, has selected Charleston as the Number One Tourist Destination in America. They listed San Francisco as number two and New York City as number three. Charleston has also been picked as America's friendliest and best mannered city. Perhaps the religious tolerance of it's people helped the city win these lofty ratings."

"Also, Fiona, as a tennis player you might be interested to note the U.S. Tennis Association has named Charleston as America's Best Tennis Town. To me there is a third reason for Charleston to be called the Holy City and that is the fact that Charlestonians have so much pride and reverence for their home town."

"Now a little geography lesson," I continued. "Charleston is located on a peninsula between the Ashley and Cooper Rivers. Charlestonians say they live where the Ashley and the Cooper Rivers meet to form the Atlantic Ocean. Both rivers were named for Anthony Ashley Cooper, the First Earl of Shaftesbury and the Chief Lord Proprietor of the Carolina Colony.

"Look. I'm sketching out a simple map to help you see the lay of the land. As an engineer sketching is important to me, you know."

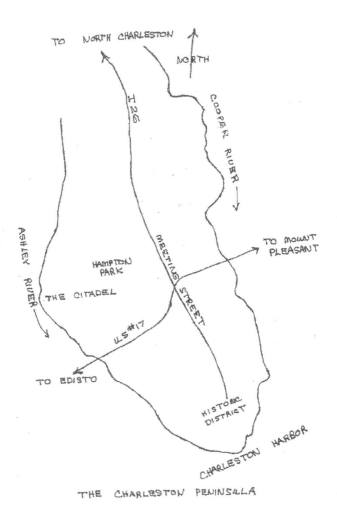

The Charleston Peninsula

Charleston Peninsula

"One of the first things you will discover in Charleston is the wonderful accent of the people. I find it to be the most attractive accent in America if not the whole world. These people are often affectionately referred to by others as 'geechees' or 'geechies.' This name is used to refer to the dialect spoken by white people in the low country (or coastal country) of South Carolina particularly between the towns of Georgetown and Beaufort. Charleston is located at the center of this region. The geechee language, sometimes called "Charlestonese," is not part of the gullah dialect spoken by the descendants of the black slaves. Certainly though it is influenced by gullah."

Fiona questioned, "Will I be able to understand them or do I need to go to language school? Will they be able to understand me?"

"There is no doubt you will have to listen closely, but I think you will soon catch on. Gullah is a Creole language based on eighteenth century peasant English but with considerable influence from various African languages. Some people say that gullah was developed by the black slaves who knew English but did not want their owners to understand what they said among themselves. When we go to Charleston I hope you will try to listen to some of the local African-Americans speaking to each other and see if you can understand what they are saying.

"You know, my mother always loves to go to Charleston. I sometimes think her favorite activity there is to go shopping and talk to the clerks in the stores just to hear their beautiful voices.

"Some people say these unusual but lovely accents are caused by something in the air. For proof of this idea they say even the crows in the vicinity of Charleston caw with a distinct geechie accent. When we get to Charleston, please listen to these birds and see if you agree with this claim. There are plenty of crows around for you to listen to."

"OK, you Sandlapper. Your mother is a lovely lady with good taste, and I know you really like this place. But birds cawing with an accent? That's getting a little carried away. Don't you think?"

Ignoring her question, I continued. "Fiona, you will be pleased to know that I have recently read that the speaking of a local dialect such as the geechee one is thought by many scholars to help old people lower their chances of mental deterioration. If you are afraid of developing such a problem, you may find it helpful to try to talk like a geechee. Charlestonians are very friendly, and they probably wouldn't get upset with your imitations of them but would smile and help you improve your pronunciations. Good luck in battling dementia."

Now Fiona was rolling her eyes.

"I think anyone planning a first trip to Charleston would do well to be familiar with some geechee words, and I want you to be prepared. Without question the language spoken in Charleston has many differences from the language spoken by other Americans. To help visitors to Charleston understand what the natives are saying, the late Frank B. Gilbreth, Jr. (a writer for *The News and Courier* newspaper, now *The Post and Courier*, and the author with his sister of *Cheaper by the Dozen*) prepared a dictionary of Charlestonese some years ago."

"Oh, I know Mr. Gilbreth's book," Fiona responded. "I did a book report on it when I was in the fifth grade. Can you

THE SKETCHING DETECTIVE AND THE SECRET ROBBERY

believe that? It was one of my mother's favorite books, and I really enjoyed it too. The movie with the same name is quite different from the book. But then movies never are as good as the book. You must get this straight, Mr. Sandlapper. We are NOT having a dozen children, cheaper or not!"

"I understand, and I'm so relieved! We could never afford twelve children. But now you are getting me away from the lesson. Listen closely. You may need this info to help you translate the gullah you are going to hear.

"Gilbreth used the name Ashley Cooper for his newspaper columns. The article referred to here is 'Lord Ashley Cooper's Dictionary of Charlestonese.'" It can be found under that name on the world-wide web. A few definitions from this dictionary are listed here:

> BECKON––meat from a pig, often eaten with a-igs for brake-fuss.
> CANE CHEW––Aren't you able to, 'Cane chew talk like a good Charlestonian?'
> MINUET––You and I have dined. 'Me and you et.'
> POET––To transfer a liquid, 'Poet it from the pitcher to the glass.'
> YAWL––Mode of address used by N'Yawkers when visiting the South."

Fiona moaned and mumbled something about her mother the grammarian.

Since nothing can dampen my enthusiasm for all things Charleston, I continued. "It has always been my belief that most people would like to see what the Garden of Eden looked like.

I suggest people visit the Charleston area during the last part of March when the millions of azaleas are in full bloom. We will do that one year. When we make that trip, you will see many Gardens of Eden in this vicinity. I'll give you a little list of Edens that will only scratch the surface."

"I do enjoy flowers and gardens, as you know. So that would be a fun visit. Even though my thumb is not very green, I can admire what other people have accomplished with plants. I might even learn a thing or two that could help our garden at home," Fiona commented. "And I won't even ask about what they wear in the Gardens of Eden since that would fluster you."

Now it was my turn to roll my eyes and sigh. But I valiantly continued my lesson. "I would particularly recommend a visit to one or more of the Charleston gardens such as the world famous Magnolia, Middleton or Cypress Gardens. However, there are many other heavenly areas to visit here such as the city's Hampton Park or White Point Gardens and many others. White Point Gardens, down by the harbor, are usually referred to as the Battery or "Bottry" by Charlestonians. That's where the cannons are. And what about going to the exceptionally lovely nearby town of Summerville? You would enjoy that too.

"Now, repeat after me. Can you say 'Bottry'?"

Fiona's attempts were feeble. She may not have much success delaying dementia after all. I thought it best to just continue our Charleston lesson.

"When we visit Charleston you may find it hard to realize that there is probably no other place in America that has suffered so many severe setbacks and yet has bounced back from each one so robustly." I numbered them off on my fingers.

1. Numerous destructive hurricanes including most recently Hurricane Hugo in 1989.
2. Large tragic fires particularly the ones of 1740 and 1861.
3. The severe earthquake of 1886 (later estimated to have been about a 7.0 on the Richter scale).
4. Blockades of the port by the pirates in 1718, the British, the Yankees, and the Nazi submarines during World War II.
5. Occupation of the city by the British and the Yankees.
6. The slave trade.
7. And many others.

"These unfortunate setbacks and the subsequent rebounds make me wonder if they played a large part in causing Charlestonians to be so innovative. Is there any city in America with more firsts than Charleston? Speaking of these firsts, the first golf course and club in the country was formed here. It was the South Carolina Golf Club formed in 1786 by local Scottish merchants in the part of the present city that was formerly called Harleston's Green. That would be 'Charleston' without the 'C'. I don't want you to think I mispronounced 'Charleston' by leaving off the 'C.' Not so. This area of the city was named for a John Harleston——with an 'H' not a 'Ch.' This was an area that was located in what is now downtown Charleston between Calhoun and Bull Streets."

Fiona did not seem very impressed by all of this so I just went on.

"Other firsts in America, though obviously of far less importance than the golf course, include:

1. The first public library (1700).
2. The first play performance (1703).
3. The first legitimate theatre (1736) now called Dock Street Theatre on Church Street.
4. The first fire insurance company (1736).
5. The first systematic recording of weather information (1737).
6. The first musical society established sometime in the 1700s. It was the St. Cecilia Society named for the patron saint of music. Since 1820 it has been a very exclusive social organization. If you would like to become a member, you will need to be a male and either your father or grandfather must have been a member. Period. These requirements mean the chances of someone becoming a member whose roots don't run deep in the city are less than nil."

"Well, I guess that leaves me out," commented Fiona. "I don't think you qualify either so our children will also be left out."

I just had to add one more item, "If you are trying to get into the St. Cecilia you must love a challenge."

"Aha!" exclaimed Fiona. "Maybe I have a chance at St. Cecilia after all. You know I am always willing to accept a challenge!"

"If that is true you might like to drive over to Augusta, Georgia and try to buy tickets to the Masters Golf Tournament. Or better yet try to figure out how the second robber took the money and got it out of the First Universe Bank."

"I just might do that very thing," warned Fiona.

"Wait though. We aren't through quite yet. There are a few more Charleston firsts you need to know about.

1. The first museum (1773).
2. The first business publication (1774).
3. The first apartment house (1800).
4. The first "fireproof building" (1823).
5. The first shot fired in the War of Northern Aggression (1861).
6. The first submarine used in combat to sink an enemy vessel (1863).
7. And many, many others, including the first department store, the first municipal college, the first prescription drug store and so on."

Fiona took a deep breath but really wasn't surprised when I kept going. She knows me and my love for Charleston so she let me continue the lesson.

"For several hundred years the prestigious place to live in Charleston has been South of Broad Street, referred to as 'South of Broad.' The architecture of the homes there is absolutely stunning. As an architect you will think you are in Camelot. A few million tourists come each year to see them. Supposedly, among other notables George Washington slept here, and Robert E. Lee visited the area.

"If you want to live in high cotton, South of Broad is the place where you will want to reside. Furthermore, you can do so if you have a few million dollars in cash sitting around doing nothing or if you are getting married to the son of one of the house owners. A quicker path might involve marriage to an elderly widower who owns one of the magnificent mansions and has no children.

"Most people think if you live on an alley in an American city, you are probably quite poor and live in a very undesirable neighborhood. That is definitely not true in Charleston, particularly if your alley is South of Broad. If you live on Price's Alley, Stoll's Alley, Bedon's Alley, Zig Zag Alley––you have really reached high cotton. By the way, Zig Zag Alley follows a path where cows used to walk.

"Look, Fiona. Here is a sketch I have done of this section of town. You can check it out and choose your alley. But remember you have to have millions stashed away if you want to buy in this neighborhood."

South of Broad

Street Map

When my architect wife saw this area for the first time, I thought she was going to go bananas. She raved on and on about what she called the Greek Revival columns and parapets, the Victorian chimneys, and other subjects equally beyond the comprehension of this ignorant civil engineer.

In my walks around Charleston I have found several cobblestone streets including South Adger's Wharf and North Adger's Wharf, both South of Broad on the east side of the city near the Cooper River. Another one is Chalmers Street located just north of Broad Street. It is the longest cobblestone street in Charleston. The Old Slave Market Museum is located at 6 Chalmers Street. I understand the cobblestone streets were built with stones brought over from England as ship's ballast.

To drive a car along one of these cobblestone streets is a very rough ride. The story goes that when a woman in Charleston is well overdue in giving birth her husband will get her in his car and drive her up and down these streets that are located only a short distance from several hospitals.

The number of fascinating places to visit in Charleston particularly South of Broad is absolutely staggering. In addition to being one of the most beautiful residential areas in America there are splendid restaurants, art galleries, antique shops, and a harbor waterfront park. Here you are, located near the center of a prosperous, bustling city, and yet South of Broad seems as quiet as a country village.

Rainbow Row is in this area where a line of eighteenth century commercial buildings have been converted to private residences. The name "rainbow" comes from the Caribbean type color scheme of the buildings. There is Longitude Lane where South Carolina's first rice was planted. You can sit in the park on a bench looking out over the harbor and see at fairly close range every ship that comes to the city as well as those that leave.

The Battle of Fort Sumter in Charleston Harbor marked the beginning of the War of Northern Aggression. After the secession of seven Southern states from the Union, the state of South Carolina demanded that the United States Army abandon Fort Sumter, but the garrison refused. An artillery barrage (from the Confederates) ensued and lasted until the fort was surrendered.

It is generally agreed that the war began on April 12, 1861, at 4:30 in the morning. Citadel cadets were stationed on Morris Island where they manned an artillery battery that shelled the fort. On April 13 the garrison on Fort Sumter took down the U.S. flag and ran up a white flag of surrender.

There were quite a few forts in the harbor at the beginning of the war. These included Fort Sumter and Fort Moultrie. Fort Sumter dominated the entrance to Charleston Harbor and was considered to be one of the strongest forts in the world at that time.

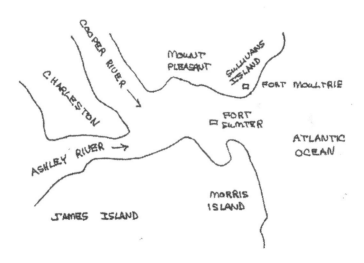

Sketch of Charleston Harbor (Here the Ashley and
Cooper Rivers meet to form the Atlantic Ocean)

Charleston Harbor

Chapter Five

The First Universe Bank

T he next morning we woke to a rainy, cloudy day and could not follow our usual schedule of swimming, walking, and fossil hunting. We had previously planned to spend bad weather days such as this one exploring the Holy City. That morning Fiona suddenly became very enthusiastic about going to the city, she said for the purpose of visiting the Charleston Market located on Meeting Street. She, however, didn't fool me as easily as she could at one time. I'm sure she was sincerely interested in seeing the Market, but it was clear to me that her main interest on that morning was visiting the First Universe Bank, also located on Meeting Street. She read in the newspaper a report on the robberies and murder at a bank she had never seen, and now she couldn't wait to go there and try to entangle herself (and me) in the investigation.

You can see what a diplomat I am when I said to Fiona, "Why don't we go over to Charleston and visit the First Universe Bank? You can 'case the joint' in your hoped for participation in solving the second robbery. Then we can visit the Charleston Market and have lunch at one of the nearby restaurants." I could see this agenda appealed very much to her.

We left soon after breakfast and drove to the north. As you come into Charleston one of the first things you will see, in addition to the great church steeples, is the Arthur Ravenel, Jr. Bridge that spans the Cooper River. Running from Charleston to Mount Pleasant it is visible from all over the city and miles around. It is the longest cable-stayed bridge in North America. This bridge has two towers or pylons and a series of steel cables running diagonally down from the towers to support the roadway at various points.

Arthur Ravenal Bridge over Cooper River (longest "cable stay" bridge in North America)

Ravenel Bridge

We drove on into the city and left our car in a parking garage near the bank. The rain had now stopped so we walked to the bank and sat on a bench across the street after I dried it off with my handkerchief. We sat staring at the bank for some time. Finally, Fiona got up, crossed the street, and slowly walked around the bank three times. I am sure as she walked she was almost praying to be allowed a chance to work on the case.

After her third trip around the building, she walked back to a Dempsey Dumpster located on the right hand side of the building where I could see it from the bench. She went up to the opening in the dumpster that is located about five feet above the ground. She leaned through the opening as far as she could and then actually climbed up into it. She seemed to me to be in a rather precarious position when all of a sudden she fell head first through the opening and disappeared from my view.

In some alarm I rushed across the street to the dumpster. When I arrived she seemed perfectly all right and was walking around inside the dumpster looking into various containers. When I realized she was not hurt, I grabbed my camera and began to surreptitiously take pictures of her in hopes I could use them later for various blackmail purposes.

I said rather sternly, "Fiona, although your exhibition of dumpster diving was superb, I think you are carrying this investigation too far. Don't you think you should come out of there right now?"

Her reply was simply, "I'm just looking around to see what sorts of things are in here." After looking around for another minute or two, she came over to the opening and said, "Help me out of this thing, Dummy."

I responded, "I'll help you out if you quit calling me Dummy or Dodo, never again speak disparagingly of my antique wood shaft golf clubs, and try never to put yourself in danger again during your crime investigations. Agreed?"

She did not reply to any of these conditions but instead piled a few boxes of trash by the opening, picked up a bag of trash, threw it at me, stepped up on the boxes then climbed up into the opening and jumped to the ground. She calmly dusted off her clothes and said, "I'm going into the bank and cash a check." She turned and strode through the front door of the bank.

A few minutes later she returned and said, "Let's head to the Market, Nincompoop. Maybe you will be able to find some of those awful golf clubs there, and perhaps I will be able to locate a bank robber and murderer." From these events you can see how well I have her trained to do my bidding.

As we walked along I said to her, "I don't know what you got out of that reconnaissance trip, but I'm sure of one thing and that is the fact that the people in the bank will remember your visit for a long time."

She seemed rather surprised and asked, "What do you mean?"

I replied by telling her that people didn't often see a magnificent freckled face girl with flaming red hair and trash stuck to the back of her skirt coming into the bank. She, not showing any embarrassment, removed the trash and said she had soaked up about all the atmosphere she could concerning the bank.

During the eighteenth century three out of four of the black slaves brought to America came through Charleston's port. Apparently many of these slaves were brought in by New England ships. Fiona is originally from Vermont, and she didn't seem to be pleased over that information. The slaves were sold at various places around the city but not at what today is often incorrectly called the Charleston Slave Market. Slaves were sold on the streets of Charleston at public auctions to the owners of the great coastal plantations for agricultural labor as well as to families for domestic service. The city officials of Charleston gave the Market to the slaves freed after the Late Great Unpleasantness. Their purpose was to allow the former slaves to have an outlet for selling their goods.

Market Hall serves as the main entrance to the Market. On the Hall's second floor the United Daughters of the Confederacy have a museum. To the rear of the Hall there are four open buildings that house roughly one hundred vendors who sell various goods and crafts. These buildings are situated between North Market Street and South Market Street. The Market opens in the morning and stays open until about 6 PM seven days per week. There you can buy just about any type of souvenir you would like to have. There are T-shirts, sketches, water colours, paintings, jewelry, books and so on. Fiona and I both were particularly interested in the sweetgrass baskets and handbags.

Market Hall

The weaving of sweetgrass baskets has been common in the Charleston area for over 300 years. This art was brought to America by the slaves from the western part of Africa. Their exquisite work is quite expensive running from a few tens of dollars for the smaller baskets up to several hundred dollars for the larger and more intricate ones. All of the work is done by hand thus no two of the baskets are exactly the same. The art of weaving sweetgrass is passed down from generation to generation and is learned as a child.

Charleston sweetgrass baskets

Baskets

The baskets were originally made from marsh grasses called bulrush. (Perhaps Moses as a baby rode on the Nile in one of them.) As time went by the weavers began to use a softer and more pliable grass called sweetgrass, a natural warm season grass that grows on the coastal sand dunes of the southeast. This grass, with its long, narrow blades is becoming more and more difficult to find because of the tremendous coastal developments of recent years. The construction work for these projects has destroyed much of the grass. Furthermore, many of the resulting housing areas are of limited access preventing the basket makers from coming to harvest the grass. It is estimated that only a few decades ago there were approximately eleven or twelve hundred families involved in the basket industry, whereas today it seems there are only 250 or 300 families involved. Thus you can see the sweetgrass basket makers are facing serious threats to their continued existence, and a treasured art form could come to an end.

In the early slave days there were large rice plantations along South Carolina's coast, and the sweetgrass baskets were much in demand for use on those plantations. Perhaps in those days the large workbaskets were the most common. They were commonly used to winnow the rice and were called "fanners." (Winnowing rice was the process of separating the grains of rice from the husks. The workers would toss the rice up into the air, and the relatively heavy rice grains would fall back into the baskets while the husks, being lighter, would be blown away by the wind. In the book of Ruth in the Bible, you will see references to winnowing grain in this manner over three thousand years ago.)

Other types of baskets were made for storing cotton, fish, grain, bread, clothes, and other items. Even the simplest and smallest of baskets may take a day or two to weave and the larger ones may require several weeks of work. Thus you can see one of the reasons for their fairly high costs. These baskets, when properly cared for, can last more than a lifetime. They may be carefully washed with a soft cloth or brush and allowed to air dry.

Sweetgrass baskets are sold at the Market and at various locations in and out of the city particularly at roadside stands along U.S. Highway 17 north of Mount Pleasant, S.C. (Mount Pleasant is quite a large suburb of Charleston located on the east side of the Cooper River.) The baskets can also be bought at a stand on Edisto Island on S.C. Highway 174 just out of Edisto Beach.

As we walked through the market we found numerous stalls where the lovely baskets were sold. In each one there was a woman or two or, on a few occasions, a man weaving the baskets. The weavers were very friendly and open to any questions. They showed us how they did the weaving and even let some children participate in the work. In setting their prices, however, they are well aware that you can't find sweetgrass baskets made anywhere else in the United States. (Baskets like these are apparently still made in West Africa.)

Fiona asked one of the weavers, "How do you get the different colors into the baskets?"

The woman explained, "We use different materials. The light yellow sections are sweetgrass, the brown is pine needles, and the dark reddish brown is bulrush. We weave them together into different patterns. The bulrush not only gives a different color but also makes the baskets much stronger."

After praising the workmanship of the women, Fiona bought two of the smaller baskets then we reluctantly left the Market. As it was already afternoon, we decided to have lunch before doing further shopping. From our reading we had selected several restaurants in the vicinity of the Market that we thought would be particularly nice to try. Unfortunately, when we checked them out we found all of the ones on our list were open only for evening meals except on weekends. Thus we decided to visit a nearby hot dog stand. I enjoyed mine fully loaded. Fiona was a little more selective.

After a brief lunch we walked the short distance over to King Street, the main street in Charleston. Among other stores on King Street there are a large number of interesting antique shops. We spent several hours going through them. Some of these places specialized in old English items such as Staffordshire pottery, others in early American furniture, and some in old military uniforms and equipment. The shop that was most interesting to me though was one with a vast collection of old sports equipment such as old tennis racquets, fishing equipment, wood shaft golf clubs, and even a collection of old golf tees.

When I was a boy I used to play golf with a delightful old gentleman named Mr. Woody who had very poor eyesight. To compensate for his bad eyesight he teed up his ball for every shot with a very long tee except when he was putting. It was rather amusing to me to see the open mouthed expressions on the faces of other golfers when Mr. Woody would tee up his ball in the fairway, the rough, and even in sand traps. He would place the ball on a tee, that was at least 4 inches long, and swing away with usually good results.

In the early days of golf it was customary for golfers completing one hole to tee off for the next hole from a spot a few club lengths from the last hole. That surely must have been nice. Sometimes on our modern American courses you have to walk or ride an eighth of a mile or more to get to the next teeing off area. (Such a feature surely must help with golf cart rentals.) In the old days at the spot where a golfer was to tee off he would take a handful of sand and build a little mound, place his ball on top of it and swing away. Sand boxes were present on each hole for this purpose. As a result, today we call tee off areas tee boxes or just tees. The work "tee" comes from the Gaelic word "tigh" meaning house.

The owner of the store told us quite a bit about golf tees. The first British golf tee patent was granted in 1889 to two Scotsmen, William Bloxsom and Arthur Douglas. Their tee consisted of a flat circular piece that had three forks or prongs sticking up. The ball was placed on top of the forks or prongs.

Tee made by Bloxsam and Douglas

From the 1890s until the 1920s hundreds of different styles of tees were used and promoted by famous players. This antique store had many of these types of tees.

Some other early golf tees

One of the problems an amateur golfer, such as yours truly, has with his golf swing is that he frequently tends to look up during his swing to see where the ball is going before the club strikes the ball. Such a practice is usually disastrous. Golfers are constantly told by their instructors to keep their eyes on the golf ball until after they hit it. This is a real and very common problem. As a result some golf tee manufacturers have attempted to address the situation (or is it undress the situation?) by making special golf tees such as the ones I've sketched here.

Golf tees made to help male golfers keep
their heads down, looking at the ball (tee?)
when they are swinging their club

I understand these tees are very helpful for many male golfers, but they seem to be of little benefit to female golfers. Fiona will not let me purchase any of these beautiful tees. I guess she just doesn't want me to improve my game because she is afraid that I'll get so much better I will be able to beat her.

If you feel these tees, said to be the most beautiful ones in the world, would help your game, you can contact GolfStuffCheaper. com to purchase them. I am somewhat reluctant to propose any special golf tees that might help women with this problem of looking up before they hit the ball.

After antique shopping it was rather late in the afternoon so we returned to Market Street for an early dinner. We picked Henry's House located only a few steps from the Market. It is said to be the oldest continuously operated bar and restaurant in South Carolina. Though the place was quite crowded, Fiona and I were able to obtain a lovely meal in a short time. Fiona ordered grilled shrimp and pasta while I had a super dish of salmon and green beans. For dessert we both chose red velvet cake.

After eating we returned to our car, paid the parking fee, and drove the forty-six miles back to our house at Edisto. On the way Fiona was extremely thoughtful. I'm sure she was using her very fine brain to try to figure out a way we could become involved in trying to solve the second robbery at the bank. Little did either of us know that we very soon were to be mixed up in the middle of the whole thing––much to Fiona's delight.

Chapter Six

The Sand Castle

As you stroll along any sandy beach you will see children from ages one to ninety digging in the sand and building forts and castles frequently with moats around them. Most of these fanciful structures built beside the ocean will be located within the usual limits of the high and low tides. As a result, the castles will probably last no more than a few hours before the tide comes along and destroys them. But they provide hours of entertainment for all of those children.

'During our frequent walks at the beach we, at Fiona's insistence, would carefully examine all of the sand construction projects we saw. This was true regardless of how small or how large the project might be. Usually the work was quite simple and unimaginative.

Every once in a while as we examined these sand structures Fiona the architect would exclaim, "The person who built this one is either an architect or should be one!" (I sometimes think she believes if you are not an architect or an architect-to-be, you are a peon and that particularly applies to civil engineers such as me.)

On almost every morning before breakfast Fiona and I would take a long walk on the beach. I'm not sure such walks by the sea are good for your waistline despite what many fitness experts claim. After you have been out walking vigorously in that wonderful sea air and return to your residence, you will find your appetite has grown to monstrous proportions. Even a dozen blueberry pancakes accompanied with piles of butter, syrup, bacon, and coffee might not be sufficient to satisfy you. After polishing off these splendid foods, you will probably start looking forward to lunch.

The sunrises at Edisto can be very spectacular with the sun coming up over the ocean to the east. To see these sunrises is well worth the loss of sleep involved. On this particular morning, however, we were not able to see the sun rise at all. It was so foggy we had trouble seeing anything more than about fifty feet away. Well, on this foggy day we had walked along the beach about a mile to the north until we were beyond the pavilion and opposite the beginning of the state park. Here there are some rather large sand dunes pretty well covered with bushes and sea oats. As we walked along, we suddenly saw a large sand castle a little distance ahead of us. The castle had a vertical pole protruding from its center. My initial thought was that it was intended to be a flag pole. Apparently this castle had been built very late on the previous day perhaps just after high tide and well up on the beach. I say this because the tide had not yet washed it away, but we were close to high tide again, and the water was coming up onto the lower edge of the castle. The part of the castle near the pole was just a jumble as though someone had shoveled the sand into a pile haphazardly.

Suddenly I heard Fiona say quite loudly, "Oh my goodness!"

In some alarm I rushed over to join her, and then I was the one saying, "Oh my goodness!"

The incoming tide had begun to take away the lower part of the castle revealing two human feet sticking out of the castle. Though I was sure a person buried in all that sand would be dead, I immediately began to dig furiously into the castle with my hands trying to uncover the person's head as quickly as possible. Fiona quickly joined me. We made short work of the sand and soon found the body belonged to a girl.

Unfortunately, after uncovering her head and upper body we could detect no breathing or pulse whatsoever. The body belonged to what appeared to me to be a slender, attractive, black-haired woman in her twenties. She was lying face down in the sand with a three pronged gig like those used for gigging flounder plunged into her back. The pole we had seen was the gig handle. The girl was wearing jogging shoes, shorts, and a short sleeved shirt. In addition, she was wearing her wedding and engagement rings, but there was nothing else on her person with which we could identify her.

Three pronged gig

This event clearly showed who wears the pants in our family. I became rather nauseous, and I'm sure my face turned as green as the island golf course. Fiona, on the other hand, seemed to be able to take the discovery of a dead body without symptoms such as mine. In a way, I think she was very excited as she surely was thinking we might be able to get involved in some way in trying to catch the perpetrator of this deed. I'm sure she was not happy this girl had been killed, but since it had happened I could clearly see she wanted to be in the midst of the investigation. She seemed almost elated. Her behavior makes me wonder how she would act if I had been the recipient of those gig prongs. I hope she would be at least a little sad as she excitedly began to try to locate my killer.

As we did not have a cell phone with us, I said to Fiona, "Why don't you run back to the pavilion, borrow the phone, and call the police and EMS telling them of our discovery. I will stay here and keep the body from being swept away by the incoming tide."

Within a very few minutes after her departure several people came over to check out the situation. "What's going on here?" an older lady asked. "Is she dead?"

"My wife has gone to notify the authorities. Please move away and stay some distance from the body so as not to disturb any of the evidence," I said trying to use a tone of authority.

In about five more minutes Fiona and two policemen arrived. By this time the girl's body was nearly covered with water, and I had to stand with one foot on her back next to the gig to keep her from being taken away by the tide. The police had been on patrol within a few blocks of our location on the beach and were able to get to the scene of the murder quite quickly. We explained to the officers how we had found the girl. After we had identified ourselves, they looked at us rather suspiciously. I think it must be wise not to discover the body of a murdered person because the police always seem to put the names of the discoverers prominently on their list of suspects.

They asked who the girl was, but we said we had no idea. No one in the gathering crowd admitted knowing her either, although one man said he thought he had once seen her jogging on the beach. The police then told us they would like to interview us later in the day at the police station when the lieutenant was available. We agreed on a time, I quite grumpily because of our apparent involvement in the case. On the other hand, Fiona was very excited and ready to go to work. From the way she looked I gathered her brain was turning over and over as she tried to figure some way to solve the murder. She was as excited as a child with a new toy. I knew in my heart she would do anything to be allowed by the police to participate in this murder investigation and in the second bank robbery in Charleston and anything else they would let her work on.

I admit I became rather depressed thinking we were going to be tied up in another dangerous murder case and have no real vacation. Fiona seemed almost gleeful about the whole thing.

At 2:00 PM we met with a Lt. Tom Seabrook at police headquarters. He was a tall serious looking man of about forty years. He was a native of Edisto Beach and a tremendous supporter of the island and its people. The idea that anyone would commit a cold blooded murder on his island within the city limits of Edisto Beach was almost beyond his comprehension.

He first told us they had quickly been able to identify the victim. He said her name was Mrs. Bobbie Mainwaring, a native of Charleston. She had been the wife of a Charleston attorney, John Mainwaring. Bobbie had been staying for a couple of weeks with some lifelong Charleston friends, Sue and Gene Manigault (pronounced MAN-e-go) at their home on Palmetto Boulevard about a mile to the south of our house. Her husband had been staying in Charleston during the week and coming to Edisto on the weekends.

By mid-morning when Bobbie had not returned from her early morning jogging, the Manigaults had begun to worry. By this time the fog had cleared so they quickly walked up and down the beach trying to find her. Having no success there, they asked their neighbors if they had seen Bobbie, but the results were the same. They then called the police to report her absence. This report was received a few hours after we reported finding the body in the sand castle. Associating the two, the police decided the body belonged to Mrs. Mainwaring.

Upon hearing the news of the death of his wife, John Mainwaring had completely broken down. Another attorney in the law firm was driving him to the island. It was reported that John could think of no reason why anyone would want to kill his lovely wife. It surely didn't appear to be a robbery because joggers rarely carry money or other valuables on their persons when they are running. As I previously said, the only valuables Bobbie apparently had with her were her engagement and wedding rings.

Lt. Seabrook asked us to carefully go over with him our observations from that morning. After this was done to his satisfaction, he said something that absolutely dismayed me. His exact words were, "We will do anything and use all our resources and anyone we can to quickly solve this dreadful murder."

The words "and anyone" were the ones that upset me so much. I knew that my red head gung-ho wife would immediately latch onto those words and say, "Use us!"

That, of course, is exactly what she did. My heart sank as she began to speak, "Would you let Jack and me try to help you find this killer? We have helped the police chief back in our hometown solve several murders in the past. Should you let us do this and should we have any luck, we will give you all the credit."

Lt. Seabrook asked for the name and phone number of our police chief (Fat Joe Reynolds). While Fiona was providing that information, my heart finished sinking. I could see our long planned leisurely vacation in the beach sunshine slipping through my fingers. All those days I had planned sunbathing, swimming, fossil hunting, afternoon naps, golfing, and so on were melting before my eyes.

The lieutenant seemed quite surprised at her words and said, "To let you do this seems a bit irregular to me since you two as finders of the body are in a way suspects yourselves. However, I'll call your police chief right now. If he says you are OK, I will give you a try."

Apparently Fat Joe gave us a glowing recommendation because as soon as the call was over Lt. Seabrook said he would let us participate in the investigation. Fiona was, of course, delighted but I was not. To me this meant our planned vacation consisting of days of loafing by the sea had gone up in smoke almost before they had started.

The lieutenant said to us, "You may work on the case, but only under my supervision. I will share information with you and will expect you to do the same for me. I will count on you to keep me informed as to your planned activities in the investigation." He smiled saying, "I will call you the Palmetto Boulevard Irregulars." As an avid fan of Sherlock Holmes, I knew exactly what he meant.

"I hope I don't need to remind you to be particularly careful with regard to your own safety. I don't want to have to pull any gigs from your backs. This killer might have a few more of those for use on anyone who gets in his or her way," a serious lieutenant told us.

Fiona asked, "Can the gig used in the murder be traced in some way to its owner?"

In reply Lt. Seabrook said, "I will look into the matter but I am not very optimistic that we will be able to trace the gig. There are probably dozens, perhaps even hundreds of gigs owned by residents of the island. We also have to consider that many visitors to Edisto bring their own gigs with them."

A favorite pastime of many people who live year round on the island and of some of the island's visitors is the gigging of flounder. Boy, is fresh flounder good to eat! Particularly if you are the one who gigged it. In most states fish gigging is legal and is usually done at night. You can either wade in the water on the edge of the shore or preferably you can quietly paddle along in a boat. Obviously, if you do this at night you will need a lantern to shine on the water to see the fish.

I said to Fiona, "The flounder settle on the bottom and, with their fins, cover themselves with sand. Often the only thing you can see of them is their eyes protruding above the sand. In addition, you may see a sort of outline of their bodies. By the way, you can get a pretty good idea as to the size of a flounder from the spacing of his eyes. If you see eyes three or four inches apart, you've located a big one. Did you know that when the flounder hatches he has one eye on each side of its brain? That is one eye is on the top of his flat body and one on the bottom. As he moves from the larval to the juvenile stage in his growth, the eye on the bottom moves to the top so both eyes are on the side that faces up.

A Flounder

"On very cold winter nights you may be able to gig saltwater speckled trout. They will come in close to the shore where you will be able to spot them. To me they seem to doze a little, but they are still very skittish. I admit that hitting one of them with a gig is beyond my capabilities. I have more luck with a big flat stationary flounder. By the way, the important item to remember here is that gigging people is not an acceptable practice in our society."

"Obviously, someone on this island missed that point about not gigging people," Fiona observed. "Now I don't consider gigging flounder as being an acceptable practice either. But I guess someone has to do the gigging if I want to enjoy flounder on my dinner plate."

The lieutenant told us he had sent two of his officers out to interview everyone staying in the vicinity of the spot where we found the body of Mrs. Mainwaring.

"They are asking these people if they had seen anyone walking down the beach carrying a gig. Actually, the murder was committed apparently right at dawn. Thus the possibility of someone seeing the killer with his gig, particularly in this morning's fog, is very slight. If they had seen someone on the beach at dawn walking along carrying a gig it would have been somewhat suspicious because most gigging is done at night and much of it back in the inland tidal creeks and rivers. The officers are also checking nearby stores where gigs are sold to see if anyone of them recently sold a three pronged gig."

Chapter Seven

Where is Bobbie Mainwaring?

Were we in for a surprise that evening! Lt. Seabrook called us after supper to say he had been knocked for a loop, and we were too when he explained the situation. It seems when John Mainwaring arrived at Edisto he immediately asked to see his wife's body. His intention was to arrange her transfer to a funeral home back in Charleston. Her body had been picked up by the Edisto EMS and taken to their headquarters on Murray Street next to the police and fire departments.

When John arrived at EMS and walked into the building, he looked quite a few years older than his actual age. He was stooped over, dragging his feet as he walked, and had tears running down his cheeks. Strangely though, a few minutes later he burst out of the building looking quite a few years younger than he had just a few minutes before. He seemed to be smiling all over. Though his face was still covered with tears, there was a spring in his step. However, at the same time he looked a little puzzled. When he had been shown the body, he shouted in great excitement, "That's not my wife. Where is she?"

The police, John, and his associate from the law firm immediately drove over to the Manigault's beach home. There Gene and Sue Manigault had been trying to mentally prepare themselves for the task of consoling their friend the best they could over his loss. When John arrived they were absolutely astonished when they saw he was almost smiling despite the fact that his young wife had supposedly just been violently murdered on the beach.

John demanded, "Where is Bobbie?"

Both of the Manigaults were just about speechless. They were finally able to mumble that she had been killed down on the beach, and her body had been picked up by EMS. John then told them that the body found on the beach did not belong to Bobbie and he again asked, "Where is my wife?"

Quite bewildered but quite happy, they said they had no idea. They further said they had not seen her since she left to go jogging before breakfast. Actually she would jog each day just at sun up.

John and the police asked to see her things in the house. They carefully examined her personal belongings and decided she had taken nothing with her other than her running clothes and shoes. Obviously, she would not have even taken her purse with her. All of a sudden this information was beginning to depress John again as he began to think that something terrible must have happened to Bobbie. Her car was still parked at the Manigaults. She apparently had no clothes other than her jogging ones and no money. Where could she have gone? I guess everyone there began suddenly to fear that she was probably dead and buried somewhere else on the island. Its sandy soil is very easy to dig in. A grave could have been dug in a few minutes almost anywhere on the island, the body tossed in, and immediately covered. Finding such a grave would be almost impossible.

In the meantime the dead girl's fingerprints were taken and sent in to be checked. As a result, it was discovered a couple of days later that her name was Martha Ulmer, a secretary for an insurance agency in Walterboro, South Carolina about forty-eight miles inland from Edisto. Martha was married to a soldier who was then stationed in Afghanistan. She was taking a week of her annual vacation and had rented an apartment on Jungle Shores Drive a few blocks from the ocean.

That evening to begin our investigation we went to the Internet to find what information we could concerning Bobbie Mainwaring and her husband. We found her maiden name was Bobbie Ravenal. She was a native of Charleston who had graduated six years ago from Agnes Scott College in the Atlanta area. After graduation she had returned to Charleston where she taught second grade for three years. Three years ago she had married John Mainwaring. Since that time she had been a housewife and worked part-time at the First Universe Bank as a secretary.

"Well, now," Fiona exclaimed. "This is an interesting bit of information. This girl, Bobbie, worked at the bank at the time of the robberies and murder. Now she has suddenly disappeared. This brings up all sorts of possibilities.

1. She may have been the second robber.
2. She may have assisted someone else conducting the second robbery.

3. She may be completely innocent but perhaps saw something or the robber thought she saw something that would identify him."

"True." I responded. "But if she was the second robber she would not have killed another girl who looked somewhat like her to try to convince the police she was dead. That would only work for a few hours before the girl's true identity was determined. I feel the last possibility in your list is the most realistic one. Perhaps the robber thinks Bobbie can identify him, but if so, why did he wait a year to try to kill her?"

"Jack," Fiona said, "don't forget no one knew there had been a second robbery until Mr. Musgrove confessed. Thus if Bobbie saw something unusual she would not have associated it with the second robbery because no one knew that a second robbery had occurred. After the Musgrove confession, however, the thing she had seen, or that the robber thought she had seen, put him in grave danger of being identified. Therefore, realizing her life was seriously threatened, she vamoosed."

Considering all of this, we had a lot to think about.

John Mainwaring, also a Charleston native, had graduated from The Citadel. (I could elaborate about this wonderful institution for many hours as I graduated from there myself, though not in the same class with John. I'll come back to this topic later.) After graduation John had spent four years in the United States Air Force Weather Service. After those years in the military he went to law school at Wake Forest University in Winston Salem, North Carolina. Upon obtaining his law degree five years ago and passing the South Carolina bar exam, he had gone to work for a well known Charleston law firm that specialized in business and corporate law as well as estate planning.

For the next several days John stayed at Edisto with the Manigaults. They, together with the police and various friends, spent those days frantically searching for Bobbie. They looked on the beach, in the stores and restaurants, in the state park RV area, and in the forests nearby. They showed photographs of Bobbie to almost everyone they met asking if she had been seen. John called the Edisto police every few hours to see if they had any news. Finally, he returned to his home in Charleston and resumed his work at the law firm. Frequently each day he checked his home and office phones to see if anyone else had called in information about Bobbie's whereabouts or better yet if Bobbie herself had called. He also continued contacting the police to ask if they had discovered anything. Of course her disappearance had been reported in all the local newspapers.

One night Fiona sat in a rocking chair on our front porch looking out in the darkness toward the ocean. At least I got in some rest and relaxation while she sat there. Sitting in a rocking chair is an old habit of hers when she wants to do some serious thinking. When she gets what she thinks is a good idea she begins to rock faster and faster. On this evening her rocking began to speed up and then suddenly she said to me that she had remembered an old friend of hers from Charleston who had gone to Agnes Scott about the same time as had Bobbie Mainwaring. Her friend's maiden name was Karen Rutledge, and now she was married to Dr. Dan Gignilliat (pronounced GIN-let).

Fiona called her friend on the phone. After chatting for a while she asked Karen if she knew Bobbie Ravenal, now

Bobbie Mainwaring. Apparently Karen knew Bobbie quite well and had been terribly shocked when she learned of her friend's disappearance. Fiona told her that we were trying to help the Edisto police find Bobbie as we had discovered the dead girl on the beach. Fiona further said she was hoping Karen could provide information to us regarding Bobbie. The net result of this conversation was that Fiona arranged to have lunch with Karen the next day at Poogan's Porch in the historic part of Charleston. Sadly, I was not invited. This was very disappointing to me as I have always loved that area of the city and take every opportunity I can to go there. I can happily spend hours wandering through the old streets looking at the magnificent restored homes, walking around Colonial Lake and sitting on a bench at the Battery looking out over Charleston Harbor. Sometimes I sit there and imagine I can see my fellow Citadel Cadets of so long ago firing their cannons at Fort Sumter. (Actually they were firing from nearby Morris Island.)

Poogan's Porch, a very fine well known restaurant, is located in a lovely Victorian house on Queen Street just to the north of the South of Broad area. I think the word "Victorian" is used to indicate the architecture of the house is of the style common during Queen Victoria's reign in England from 1837-1901. I don't think the word has anything to do with the number of children women had in those days. Queen Victoria had nine children and 42 grandchildren.

The restaurant was named for Poogan, a scruffy looking dog. The porch of this lovely house seemed to be his favorite resting place as he wandered around the nearby neighborhood. In the front yard there is a grave marker for Poogan. The restaurant is quite famous for its wonderful low country food and for the considerable number of celebrities who have dined there.

After enjoying lunch and much conversation, Fiona returned to the beach late in the day with some information she thought might be helpful in our investigation. Karen had told her that about a year ago Bobbie had been working at the First Universe Bank when it was robbed. The robber came into the bank with a stocking mask over his head and a pistol in his hand to make an illegal withdrawal. He instructed Bobbie and several other employees and customers to lie face down on the floor.

When the robber demanded money from one of the tellers, that teller refused and the robber shot and killed him. The other tellers quickly handed over most of the cash they had on hand. The robber then told one of the secretaries to get up from the floor. When she did so he told her to go into the safe and fill the bag with large bills. She did as she was told. After this robbery and murder, John Mainwaring told Bobbie he felt she should no longer work in the bank as it was too dangerous. She reluctantly gave notice and two weeks later left the bank.

Chapter Eight

Another Trip to the First Universe Bank

T he next day when we learned the name of the group that insured the bank, we were quite pleased because we had performed an investigation rather successfully for them on another case two years ago. As a result of this association and our new relationship with Lt. Seabrook, we were given permission to visit the bank and interview its president, Mr. James Rivers. One afternoon a few days later we made a trip to Charleston to see him.

We arrived at the bank right in downtown Charleston. As soon as we entered the building we walked over to one of the tellers. She wished us good morning and said she remembered the girl with the magnificent red hair who cashed a check a few days before. She politely didn't mention the trash on the back of Fiona's skirt. Fiona almost blushed but, as I mouthed the words, "I told you so," she thanked the teller and asked if we could speak to Mr. Rivers. She explained we were the MacKays and had an appointment with him. The teller went into the president's office and quickly returned to tell us to go right in. We entered the office where we were greeted pleasantly by a tall thin man with a hawk nose who was probably in his early forties. Although his welcome was quite cordial my attention was immediately diverted to an old wood shaft golf club hanging on the wall behind his desk. I had never seen one of this type before, but from my frequent references to various antique golf club books, I instantly recognized it as a swan neck club promoted by P.A. Vaile of New Zealand. This type of club never caught on, thus only a few of them were ever made. I was so excited I almost jumped up and down.

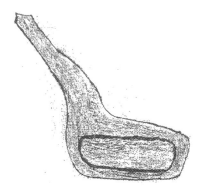

A swan neck brassie (thats a #2 wood) from New Zealand

Swan Neck Golf Club

Upon seeing my excitement over the club, Mr. Rivers said to me, "It's yours if you successfully get to the bottom of this mystery."

I jokingly asked, "Even if you are the robber?"

He laughed and replied, "Yes, even if it's me."

While I was covetously looking at the swan neck golf club, Fiona was excitedly examining a large number of old wooden tennis racquets located in several glass cases along the walls of Mr. Rivers' office. There were over one hundred of them. During the previous two years she had begun collecting old tennis items, particularly racquets. The way she carries on when she finds some of these broken down racquets causes me to feel she is making fun of my great love for those old, beautiful, lovely, gorgeous, wonderful wood shafted golf clubs that I collect.

Today she was acting like an idiot oohing and aahing over some useless, crummy, ugly old tennis racquets. Some of these racquets were bent and had broken strings—just a pile of junk in my opinion. I do admit some of them had the oddest looking shapes I have ever seen. Mr. Rivers, seeing how much she admired those racquets, said if we solved the case not only could we have that beautiful golf club, but we could have any four of the tennis racquets in the cases. I can't imagine why anyone would want those sorry looking things. I thought they might make good wood to burn in my fireplace the following winter. I really thought we should ask him if he had any other old wood shaft golf clubs at his home that we could have instead of those useless racquets. But then if I did ask that question, Fiona would probably rip that wonderful swan neck golf club from the wall and bend it over my head.

The early history of tennis is quite hazy. Some people claim the ancient Egyptians, Greeks, and Romans played a game somewhat similar to the tennis of today. To back up their claims these people say the word "tennis" was derived from the name of an Egyptian town named Tinnis that is located along the Nile River. They further claim the word "racquet" was derived from the Arabic word "rahat" that stands for the palm of the hand. Indeed, the palm of the hand was used to hit tennis balls many centuries later in France, Italy, and England. Other than those two words, "Tinnis" and "rahat," investigators have so far failed to find any direct evidence to indicate the game was played by people in the Middle East before it was played in western Europe.

It has been verified tennis was played in France by monks perhaps as early as the eleventh or twelfth centuries. At that time the game was apparently quite similar to handball in that the ball was hit up against a wall. Later the ball was hit over a net. At first the balls were struck with their hands. Jeu de paume was a French game played with the palms of the hands. The words "jeu de paume" mean "a game of the palm." As hitting the balls with the hands was uncomfortable, the players began to use gloves and later wooden paddles. In the 1500s players began to use wooden frame racquets with sheep gut strings. The Italians are usually said to be the ones who originated these racquets.

I sketched two lop-sided jeu de paume racquets as I thought about how ugly they are. I don't really know how a racquet this shape helped a player nor do I know how anyone came up with this idea for a racquet to be shaped this way. I would guess that a Frenchman was playing doubles one day with his wife as his partner. All of you male tennis players realize this is a dangerous practice. Very probably she struck him on the head bending her racquet into the shape shown. After this minor incident in her life she may have continued playing with the bent racquet and found she liked to hit balls with it. It may have helped her in some manner with her lobs. (I wonder what this lady did later when she wanted another lop-sided racquet. Do you guess she bent it just as she did the first one? I bet so.) By the way, not all jeu de paume racquets were lop-sided.

Two Jeu de Paume racquets from the 1700s

Jeu de Paume Racquets

In recent years a sport called beach tennis has been played by more and more sun lovers on beaches around the world. In this game the players have either paddles or tennis racquets and use them to hit the ball back and forth across a net to courts of specified dimensions. At Edisto we love a very informal version of this game that involves striking the ball with our hands (jeu de paume?) back and forth across a line drawn in the sand to serve as a net. We make up our own rules and mark out the court of a size that suits us. The only equipment we use is a tennis ball or a sponge rubber ball, whichever is on hand. The game is a great deal of fun and involves much exercise and many joking insults tossed back and forth. While you are playing this rather noisy game, many strangers walking along the beach will come over to watch. Often they will ask if they may join us, a request that we usually happily grant.

Here are sketches of several of the old wooden tennis racquets Mr. Rivers had in his office. Since the 1980s racquets have been made with non-wood composites. The old ones such as the I have sketched were made with wood frames.

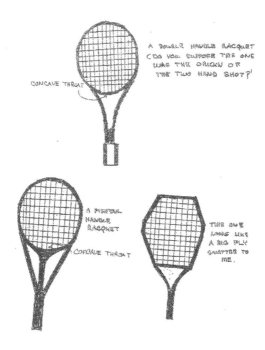

Some early 20th century wood handle tennis racquets

Some Early 20th Century

The next racquet was also made in the 1880s. It has a rain drop or tear drop shaped face and a convex throat. Convex throats were often used for racquets made from the 1880s on into the 1920s. When Fiona sees a racquet with a convex throat at garage sales or flea markets, she grabs it. These throats are one indicator that racquets are probably fairly old.

A tear drop shape racquet from the
1880s with a convex throat

Another one of Mr. Rivers' racquets and one that is not very
old is the Bjorn Borg all wood racquet made in the late 1970s
or early 1980s by Donnay of Belgium. I wonder if I had one
of these if I could hit the tennis ball like Borg could and can.
(What beautiful top spin shots and super backhand shots he
hits. Actually that can be said of all his shots.)

Donnay Borg tennis racquet

Mr. Rivers told us something of tennis racquet manufacture in the last several decades.

"In the 1970s and early 1980s racquets were commonly made from wood, metal or composites. However, the success of metal racquets in the early 1970s soon led to the manufacture of racquets with materials other than wood or metal. Today most racquets are made with a carbon fibre called graphite," he explained.

We eventually settled down and began to discuss the robbery and murder with Mr. Rivers. He seemed just as shocked as anyone that the robber said he had obtained only $110,000 in the robbery. He thought Mr. Musgrove had taken the whole $600,000 and had hidden the rest of it somewhere. He was dismayed when he realized that he and the other employees of the bank were looked on with great suspicion by the people of Charleston, particularly the bank customers. Mr. Rivers told us a representative of the insurance group had expressed considerable approval when he heard we were going to be working on the case.

I asked Mr. Rivers, "Does the bank always have this much cash sitting round?"

He replied, "Not usually. Only near the first of each month when the employees of several companies in the vicinity of the bank come in to cash their pay checks. So we arrange to have a very large supply of cash on hand at those times."

My next question followed. "Did most of the $600,000 missing come from the tellers' booths or from the bank's vault?

He considered my question. "Well, I would guess for the $110,000 taken by the first robber about half came from the tellers and about half from the vault. For the second robbery I think most of it came from the vault."

Fiona asked if the first robber had gone into the safe himself. Mr. Rivers said the robber had not entered the safe but rather had produced from his pocket a cloth bag and ordered one of the bank secretaries to go into the safe and fill the bag with used $20, $50, and $100 bills. (I assume the thief was thinking the bank would not have any records of the serial numbers of circulated bills. Such might not be the case for new bills.)

As the young lady started toward the safe, the robber said, "If you close the safe or lock yourself in it, I will shoot your friends here in the lobby." She wisely did neither of those things.

We asked Mr. Rivers if we could speak to that secretary if she still worked at the bank. He said she did still work there and stepped out of his office for a few minutes. While he was gone I examined the New Zealand golf club in great detail while Fiona was drooling over the cases of old tennis racquets. When Mr. Rivers returned he brought with him a small, very attractive black haired woman of about twenty-nine or thirty years. He introduced her as Mrs. Maria Prioleau (pronounced PRAY-low). By her beautiful accent it was obvious she was a Charleston native. When I asked her if Prioleau was a French Huguenot name, she replied that her husband was a Huguenot and since her marriage she had attended the Huguenot church on Queen Street in the city. I understand this is the only Huguenot church operating in America today. It was founded in about 1681 by French Huguenot refugees fleeing the persecution of Protestants back in France.

In response to our questions concerning the robbery, she said with the prompting of the robber she rushed into the safe and quickly filled the bag with ten and twenty dollar bills. She only included a few fifty and one hundred dollar bills in an attempt to minimize the bank's loss as much as possible. When she came back out of the safe she handed the bag to the robber who told her to lie face down on the floor. He then rushed out the front door of the bank and disappeared.

"Mr. Rivers," I asked, "where were you and what did you do during and after the visit by the armed robber on that fatal morning?"

He responded, "I was sitting at the desk in my office going over some proposed advertising we were planning to use for the bank. Suddenly I heard what sounded like a pistol shot. I rushed into the main area of the bank. As I did this, I was immediately accosted by a masked man who came over to me and jabbed a pistol into my stomach. He shouted, 'Lie face down on the floor as these other people are doing or you won't live but a few more seconds.' I did as I was told.

"As soon as the robber left the bank, I instructed a teller to call 911 to notify the police and to ask EMS for an ambulance. I said to all the bank customers that they must stay in the bank until the police arrived. Also, I asked the tellers to carefully count the money they had remaining."

As we were leaving Mr. Rivers' office I asked if we could walk around the bank and introduce ourselves to each of his employees. He said that would be fine and then I made one final remark. "Please take good care of that golf club and those tennis racquets. We hope to return in the near future and collect them." He smiled and said he would keep them under lock and key.

Fiona and I then moved around the bank introducing ourselves. We met Mr. George Mengedoht (pronounced men-GEE-dot) the vice-president, each of the tellers, secretaries, assistants to the president, and the janitor. We asked each one of these persons if they had any idea how the second robbery was committed. They all said they had no idea. We then asked each of them to notify us if they later had any ideas or suggestions as to how the crime was carried out. After these interviews and on our way back to Edisto, Fiona and I agreed that not a single one of the bank employees seemed reticent to speak to us and not one of them seemed to be hiding anything. They appeared to be as bewildered as we were as to how the second robbery was committed.

Fiona said to me, "I know you meant well when you asked that we be allowed to meet all of the bank employees to question them and tell them what we were doing. However, you must realize if one of them is the second robber and the person who killed Martha Ulmer on the beach, you have made us into a bull's eye for him."

By the time we finally left the bank it was quite late in the afternoon so we decided to have an early supper at Henry's House. That evening we wanted to catch one of the ghost walks that begin in the neighborhood near the Charleston Market. We did not have a reservation, but they had a few spots left and allowed us to purchase tickets.

To me one of the most fascinating things you can do while visiting Charleston is to take one of the numerous ghost walks that are offered. Interest in such tours around our country has never been higher. This fact is particularly obvious in Charleston where so many such walks are available. They begin at various points in the old part of the city, down at the Battery by the harbor, over on Calhoun Street, by the Market, and at other places. The walks generally run for about one and one half hours.

Ghosts seem to like ocean air and are particularly numerous in old seaside cities such as Boston, Charleston, New Orleans, Philadelphia, and Savannah. The historic places in those cities seem to be particularly attractive to ghosts. I guess those places, having been around for long periods of time, have provided the ghosts plenty of time to move in.

Do you believe in ghosts? Well, maybe you don't, but I'm willing to bet if you don't believe in them and yet you take one of the Charleston ghost walks you will have some second thoughts on the matter before your tour is over. Also, when you return to your lodging that evening, I bet you will look under your bed and into your closets several times before you retire.

Many people in the know say that Charleston is America's most haunted city, but the fact is that several other cities make the same claim. Anyway, there are apparently at least 18 identifiable ghosts who make Charleston their permanent home.

It was after dark when we began our particular tour. I was soon to discover that the best part of our walk was the pleasant and knowledgeable young male guide who led and lectured us on the subject of the unknown. He was very well versed in Charleston history, and he cheerfully and patiently answered all the questions from our group. Even though we did not encounter a real ghost on our trek, we had lots of fun listening and questioning our talented guide.

Though the most haunted single place in Charleston is said by many to be the Dock Street Theatre located on the corner of Church and Queen Streets, it seemed to me that overall the largest total number of those beings are located in the old houses of the city. According to our guide, quite a few of the ghosts in these houses met their fate while they were humans in very unfair circumstances. Perhaps they had returned to the human realm to try to right those situations. On many occasions if those situations were rightfully handled, the ghosts usually went away and never returned.

On our particular tour we first walked to Poogan's Porch. The dog Poogan is now dead and gone, but a lady named Zoe St. Amand who lived in the house and supposedly died there in 1954 is said to frequently be seen looking out of the windows of the house. Maybe she decided to stay there in her afterlife because of the fifteen thousand bottle wine cellar the house is said to contain. We visited a hidden cemetery, walked by the Carriage House to look for a headless ghost who is said to reside there, stopped by the old city jail (a very haunted place), and walked among the great live oak trees at the Battery looking for the ghosts of various pirates. In the 1720s, twenty-nine pirates were reportedly hanged from these trees. Apparently they were left hanging there for some days. Some people have claimed in recent years to have seen them still hanging there after dark.

Once we completed the tour and returned to our house at Edisto, I, being very brave, looked under my bed only three times. It is true that on two occasions during the night I did get up to check the door and window locks and examine the contents of our closets.

Chapter Nine

Dumpster Diving

How did the second thief get the money out of the bank without being discovered? We thought that would have been an extremely difficult task to carry out without being caught and arrested even though the police and the bank employees thought the robbery was over. The big robbery apparently occurred after the first robber had left the bank. Any money that was later discovered to be missing was credited to the man who committed the first robbery and shot the teller. The police had spent this last year trying to find the first robber not realizing there was a second one. They, nor anyone else, ever dreamed another robber, perhaps a bank employee, was going to steal an even larger sum of money right in front of their eyes.

The second robber was quite an opportunist because he realized he could steal a great deal of money immediately after the first robbery with little chance of getting caught. No one ever dreamed someone else was going to sneak a bundle of money out from the bank with the police all over the place. This was a splendid time for a robbery because any money that turned up missing would be blamed on the first robber. The major danger would be in getting the money out of the bank.

The second robbery was so smooth it was as though nothing had happened. If it hadn't been for the deathbed confession of Mr. Musgrove it is probable the second robbery would never have been discovered.

Fiona and I decided we would spend our first efforts trying to learn how the money was removed from the bank. After considerable talk and discussion we agreed there were three ways it might have been done.

Our first idea was that the second robber grabbed a large pile of bills, stuffed them into a trash sack and threw it into a trash can that was later carried to the dumpster. Such a procedure would necessitate a moonlight trip by the robber to the dumpster located in the rear of the bank as well as some "dumpster diving." This visit would probably have occurred on the night of the robbery before the city trash crews emptied the dumpster as they do every two or three days. The practice of dumpster diving does not, as the words seem to suggest, physically involve diving into a dumpster as Fiona had done a few days before. Dumpster diving is the practice of sifting through residential or commercial trash. This practice, called "skipping" in the UK, may actually involve some climbing into and out of the dumpsters.

Should the second robber have been seen that night by the night watchman, he probably would have told the watchman he was looking for a misplaced item such as a glove or sweater or something else and nothing would have been thought about it. As we thought along these lines, we began to wonder if someone other than the janitor might have observed the diving operation and if that person could have been Bobbie Mainwaring.

Even if someone had observed the second robber at the dumpster, he or she would probably have no suspicions about the incident because at that time no one knew there had been another robbery. The first robber took the money and left by the front door. In fact, it was almost a year later before the second robbery was discovered when Mr. Musgrove made his deathbed confession. But what if someone did see a dumpster diver on the night of the robberies? Last year on that night no one other than the second robber knew there had been a second robbery. If on that night he had gone to the dumpster to retrieve the money he had somehow placed in the trash and was seen by one of the bank employees, he would not have worried about the matter. But now that the second robbery was public knowledge, the robber might begin to think the person who saw him could associate his diving with the second robbery. If all this was true, could the person who saw him have been Bobbie Mainwaring? If so, he might have decided to eliminate her to be on the safe side.

The second way in which we thought the money could have been removed from the bank involved the use of the United States Postal Service. A few hundred thousand dollars in twenty and larger bills could quickly and easily be fitted into one of the post office's custom shipping boxes measuring 12"x12"x5 ½" and mailed to the thief's home address or to some other address.

In a similar manner the cash might have been shipped to a certain person by the United Parcel Service or by Federal Express. It is my understanding that these two excellent companies will not deliver to PO Box numbers. They deliver only to known residences or businesses.

We next decided to investigate each of the three possibilities of removing the money from the bank. With the approval of Lt. Seabrook and James Rivers we drove to North Charleston that afternoon to interview the night watchman at his home. We asked him if, on the night of the robbery, he had noticed anyone visiting the bank's dumpster.

In answer he said, "I usually spend most of my working time inside the bank and only check outside one or two times each night. Each of those checks only lasts for a few minutes. I did not notice anyone coming to the dumpster the evening of the robbery. However, most of my nighttime work is in locations where I cannot not see the dumpster. During the ten years I have worked at the bank I have sometimes seen people looking into or reaching into the dumpster. Some of the people actually climb into it. But I think they are looking for food, and I certainly would not try to prevent them from doing that. I do know some people who visit the dumpster are collectors of old things or other items that have some kind of value. These people regularly visit all the dumpster sites in the city. There is one lady and her daughter, both named Mary, who visited the site regularly. I let them look as they please since they are probably harmless. I admit I am entertained by their excitement when they find something they call a 'treasure.'" He smiled thinking about the two Marys.

Fiona and I thought one or more of the other bank employees might have come to work on the night of the robbery and may have observed some dumpster diving. We, together with President Rivers, asked every single employee of the bank if they had been to the building that night and had observed any divers. Not one of the people working for the bank at that time said they had returned on the night of the robberies.

The thought occurred to us that a year ago there might have been someone working for the bank who was no longer employed there or who was on vacation or sick leave. The president and his secretary went through their records in detail and found only one person who fell in that category, Mrs. Bobbie Mainwaring. This was rather surprising to us and it was going to be rather difficult to interview her since no one knew where she was or whether or not she was still alive.

Then we had another thought. Maybe Bobbie had either seen someone stuffing money into an envelope, post office shipping box or trash bag and /or had later seen someone going to the dumpster that evening to retrieve something. If either of these situations or both had occurred she would probably have thought nothing of it at the time. But now she had surely learned there was a second robbery, and she had just narrowly escaped being murdered with a gig. She now surely feels the robber knows she saw him doing something suspicious on the day of the robbery. As a result, we speculated she had decided to disappear because she thought she now knew the identity of the second robber who was wise to her. At that time we clearly were of the opinion that the robbery had been committed by a person who had used the trash sack method in getting the money out of the bank or who had used one of the mailing services to get it out.

On the suggestion of Lt. Seabrook, the Charleston police visited the main post office to ask if they had picked up any packages from the bank on the day of the robberies and murder or on the next day. However, their records were insufficient to answer the question. When the police visited the offices of UPS and FedEx they found those companies had no records of deliveries or pickups at the First Universe Bank on either of the two days in question.

We then asked Mr. Rivers to provide the names of the persons who had access to the bank vault. He replied that all the tellers did and in fact so did every one else in the bank other than the janitor. We said that must mean just about anyone could go into the vault at almost any time during the day without supervision and stuff a box or envelope full of money. He agreed and upon further questioning said their bank did not have a camera in the vault to keep track of those coming and going.

This discussion reminded me of a case Fiona and I had worked on where the money stolen from a bank was hidden in a safe deposit box at that very bank. As a result, I asked Mr. Rivers if that could have been a possibility in this case.

His reply was, "That thought occurred to me and I mentioned it to the police who looked into it. The thief would have had to pick up the money elsewhere in the bank, carry it to the safe deposit vault, and put it into his or her box. The police were furnished with a list of people who went to their boxes on the day of the robbery. The list was not very long because to store the volume of bills taken in the second robbery would require quite a large safe deposit box. This fact substantially reduced the number of boxes that needed to be checked. They persuaded each of those people and each of our employees who had boxes here to open them without a court order. The police examined them all and found no trace of the missing $490,000."

He continued, "But the thief has had a year to get the money out of the bank. It may have been put in one of the boxes then, but he may very well have removed a little of it at a time over the months since. If this was the case, probably all of it has been removed by this time."

Chapter Ten

The Citadel

We had been visiting the bank and speaking to its president. As we were getting into our car to leave, I suggested we run by my alma mater, The Citadel. I hadn't been there in some months, and I'm always very excited when I have an opportunity to visit the school. I was particularly delighted on this occasion when I found Fiona was quite agreeable to such a trip.

As we approached the college I drove into Hampton Park, an area that adjoins the eastern side of the campus. I wanted Fiona to see this lovely area where I had walked so many times on weekends when I was a cadet. During those days there was a human skull up on a high limb in one of the tall trees. Some people said it was the skull that played a large part in Edgar Allan Poe's classic story "The Gold Bug." In the story the bug was made from real gold. Actually the events described by Poe took place over on Sullivan's Island and the adjacent mainland and not in Hampton Park. Sullivan's Island is located across the Cooper River to the east of Charleston along the entrance to Charleston Harbor. It was the scene of a famous battle with the English during the Revolutionary War. In Poe's story a skull was found on a high limb up in a large tree. The bug was dropped through the place in the skull where the left eye had been located. From the point where the bug hit the ground certain distances were measured and a buried treasure was located. I have always loved Poe's wonderful story and have looked up into many large trees wondering if some day I will see a skull in one of them that will lead to treasure.

After walking for a while in the park we returned to our car and drove onto the nearby campus of the very strict military college. During the first few weeks of the fall semester a fair number of freshmen leave the school. I guess the clanging of the iron gates being closed each night locking them in and the disciplined life each cadet has to live are not their piece of cake.

I'm sure a large percentage of the entering students each fall initially have some misgivings and ask themselves, "What have I done coming to this prison?" I surely fell into that class and asked myself, "Why in the world didn't I go to a university somewhere?"

However, after that initial period is over, the retention rate in the cadet corps and the later graduation rate are amazingly high among American institutions of higher learning. Furthermore, those who stay seem to soon develop an extraordinary love and devotion for the school and they keep it for the rest of their lives. I guess esprit de corps imperceptibly sneaks up on you. I am always amazed at the number of cadets in my class who almost left during those early weeks but later became the most avid supporters of the school.

I have always thought most college campuses are very attractive and well maintained, and I like visiting them. If you have never been to a military campus such as The Citadel I think you are in for a pleasant surprise when you observe the symmetry of the building layouts and see how the buildings blend so beautifully together.

There is an old saying at institutions of higher learning that if the buildings on a college campus go well together, the school does not have an architecture department. (There, on behalf of the Civil Engineering profession I got in one shot at those crazy architects like Fiona.) Anyway, The Citadel doesn't have an architecture curriculum; the buildings do blend together quite beautifully and symmetrically; and the grounds are immaculate.

There is another old saying that I just made up to the effect that if parents could select the college they would like their children to attend, The Citadel would have a million new students each year. My father sent my brother and me there, I think, because he thought the military training would straighten us out. (My brother clearly needed this straightening.)

Fiona and I entered the campus at the Main or Lesesne Gate and turned right onto the Avenue of Remembrance. We passed Summerall Chapel and stopped at Mark Clark Hall for a chocolate milk shake. My financial situation as a cadet was such that I could purchase just one of those delicious shakes every two weeks. This I did on alternate Friday afternoons after the week's classes were over, and we had marched in the Friday afternoon parade. How I looked forward to those occasions! I would slowly savor the shakes to make them last as long as possible.

After this pleasant stop I led Fiona out the front door of the hall and across the street onto the parade ground for further reminiscing. As we walked, I told her about our Friday afternoon parades during the school year. Unfortunately, it was summer at the time of our visit, and we were not able to witness one of those events. These weekly parades are said to provide the best free shows in Charleston.

I think anyone who appreciates band music and military marching would love to attend these parades. I think the most exciting part is the bagpipe and drum band. This band performs at Highland games all over the United States and has even performed in Edinburgh, Scotland at their annual world famous Tattoo. At our Friday parades we also had the regular marching band with its horns and drums. This band marches right behind the pipe band.

As we walked along I could hear in my memory the bands playing and the sounds of the cadets' marching feet coming along the street behind the grandstand. I marched in so many of these parades that I think the "Washington Post March" and "Stars and Stripes Forever" worked their way into my bloodstream. Often as I walk down the street in any town, I find myself unconsciously whistling the tunes of these marches.

As a cadet I loved the parades except for one thing––the occasional visits made by bees or horseflies with their great big sharp teeth. For the parades we were, of course, in our uniforms wearing white gloves. If one of those stinging insects lit on your face or neck, all you could do was try to blow him off. Your fellow cadets around you could not help either. If your pals behind you saw a bee or horsefly light on your neck, all they could do was to blow as hard as they could but to no avail. You had your rifle in one hand, and if you took your other hand and slapped at a bug everyone in the crowd would see the movement of the white glove. The result for you would be numerous demerits plus having to march a good many tours. Tours consist of hours of your weekend free time spent marching back and forth on the courtyard or quadrangle of your barracks with your rifle on your shoulder. We the cadets, or that is the marchers, put on so much insect repellant before the parades that we called them the citronella parades.

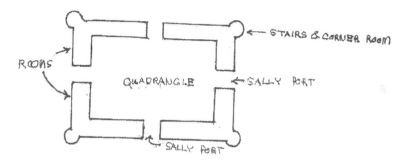

Sketch of one of the Citadel Barracks

Barracks

As I described the parades to Fiona, I led her on a walk diagonally across the parade ground to the grandstands erected for viewing in front of Padgett-Thomas Barracks. We sat there in the stands for a while as I talked to her about my cadet days. I am sure she would have been thrilled as I always am to hear the pipes and drums of the pipe band as well as the horns and drums of the regular marching band.

After a while I led her over to the civil engineering building, LeTellier Hall, to see if any of my old professors were around. Fortunately, Major Bert Frampton was in his office and seemed pleased to see one of his former students. He had taught several of my structural courses. Being a great admirer of his, I was delighted to see him.

I introduced him to Fiona and told him she was one of those people who cause frequent troubles for civil engineers as she was an architect. Despite this fact, he greeted her quite warmly and asked an inappropriate question as to how she got tangled up with this dodo. (Do you think he was speaking of me? He may not have been as great a professor as I thought.) Then he said to Fiona, "I sure am sorry you didn't come to our school and take civil engineering. Now that we have girls in the cadet corps you would have helped considerably in brightening up the scenery around here."

Disregarding his negative comments about me, I told him how much I had enjoyed his class. He was such a wonderful professor that each day after his lectures on structural steel design, reinforced concrete design or structural analysis, I would come out of class saying to myself, "That's what I want to do when I graduate from college." He influenced so many of us to follow in the structural field that we are often called, "Bert's Boys" among engineers in the southeast. When I told him how proud I was to be included in the list, his eyes seemed to fill with tears.

I told him we were having a very pleasant vacation for a few weeks at Edisto Beach. I admitted we were the people who found the girl on the beach who had been murdered with the flounder gig. I explained how we had become involved in the murder investigation and how we were trying to help the police locate the missing girl, Bobbie Mainwaring. When I mentioned her name, he said he knew the Mainwarings quite well and had been on quite a few hunting trips with John Mainwaring.

He mentioned several expeditions he had made with John when they had gone to an island owned by the Mainwarings located southwest of Edisto well out in the salt marshes. He explained how going to this very isolated and seldom visited island was a little difficult because you could only get there by the salt creeks at just about full high tide.

Fiona and I perked right up when the Major mentioned Mainwaring Island and an old house or hunting lodge there. We both had the same thought—maybe Bobbie went there to hide if she had not been killed or kidnapped. We told him we would like to visit the island in the off chance Bobbie might be hiding there and asked him to please tell us how to get there. He replied that he would do better than that. He walked over to a filing cabinet, rumbled around in it for a while and finally found a United States Geological Survey map of the marshes below Edisto Island. He gave it to us after he indicated where the island was located and which creeks we needed to travel to reach the island. After thanking him for not only the map and directions but also for the kindness and patience that he showed me and my fellow cadets, we took our leave and headed back to Edisto. We both were very excited thinking we may have stumbled over Bobbie's hiding place if she was still alive.

Chapter Eleven

Mainwaring Island

On our return to Edisto we reported to Lt. Seabrook there was a possibility Bobbie Mainwaring might be hiding over on an island in the marshes southwest of Edisto Beach. We told him where we had obtained this idea, and he seemed quite interested in the possibility of finding her there.

After thinking about our suggestion for a minute or two, he mused, "Suppose she is alive and hiding there from the person who killed the girl on the beach. We, of course, would like to talk to her, but at the same time we don't want the killer to know where she is hiding because that might mean he would go over there and try to kill her."

He continued, "Since tomorrow is Saturday and I am not on duty, why don't we go on a fishing trip in the general area of Mainwaring Island. We can troll up and down near the entrance to the creeks that go back through the marshes and to the island. At about one and a half hours before high tide, we can start up the creek and try to make our way to the place. During that time we will be on constant lookout for anyone who might be following us. If we see no one we can start up the creek and make our way to the island. Hopefully, once there we will have a full two hours to search the area without getting stranded when the tide goes out."

After consulting a tide table he said, "High tide will occur at the island about 11:40 tomorrow morning. Let's plan to be ready to leave the dock at my house on the South Edisto River by 8:00 AM. I will have plenty of fishing tackle on board for the three of us. Be sure to come prepared by wearing long-sleeved shirts, pants and sun hats. If you stay out on the water for most of the day at Edisto and are not used to it, the sun can burn you to a crisp. Bring plenty of sun tan lotion, insect repellant, and water. If we don't get a good sea breeze on the rising tide tomorrow morning, the insects back in the swamps will come out and make mince meat of us if we are not prepared for them—that is soaked in insect repellant. I will get my wife to prepare a picnic lunch for us and Mrs. Mainwaring too if she is on the island." The lieutenant then gave us directions to his house located on Palmetto Drive where it runs along the shore of the south fork of the river.

Fiona then said, "We, of course, don't know if Bobbie will be there, but if we do find her she is probably starving for fresh meat (other than fish), butter, milk, fruit, and vegetables. I will bring some of those items in case we are able to find her. Another thing she may not have is insect repellant so I'll throw in an extra bottle or two of that."

The next morning we arrived at Lt. Seabrook's home at the appointed time, loaded our things into his runabout and started across the river. The Edisto is the longest (206 miles) undammed, unleveed, black-water river in North America and perhaps in all the world. By 8:30 we had crossed the South Edisto and begun to troll with artificial lures along the edges of the marshes near Pine Island. During the next hour and a half we passed Pine Island on the ocean side and gradually worked our way into Fish Creek getting closer and closer to our ultimate destination. As we didn't catch anything trolling, we anchored the boat near the marsh and began to still fish using shrimp for bait. Much to my surprise we then caught several summer speckled trout and one of my favorite fish, a flounder.

After a while, having seen no other persons who might be following us, we continued up Fish Creek between Pine Island and the Otter Islands. Shortly after ten o'clock Lt. Seabrook decided the tide was sufficiently high for us to begin moving to our destination. We pulled in our fishing lines and the boat anchor before moving west into the smaller and shallower Jefford Creek. We began to inch our way along its twisting and turning path. Occasionally, the propeller of our outboard motor would touch bottom. However, we did not have to stop, and the water was gradually getting deeper as the tide came in. We passed the Otter Islands and moved to a little bit south of Fenwick Island. We were now out in an ocean of marsh grass. After some time of this slow travel we came around a sharp curve in the creek and saw a wooded island several hundred yards ahead. This was Mainwaring Island.

Lt. Seabrook immediately stopped his boat's motor and in a very soft voice said to us, "If Mrs. Mainwaring is on the island we don't want to give her advance warning of our arrival. We will float and paddle the rest of the way and speak as little and as quietly as possible. Apparently she believes someone is trying to find and kill her. Should she be on the island and hear us coming, she will surely run and hide.

"This is a fairly large island covered with a jungle-like growth that provides innumerable hiding places. We will have only about two hours on the island before we have to leave because of the falling tide. To find someone hiding back in the forest might take several days."

The paddling was not difficult because the incoming tide did most of the work carrying us slowly and silently to our destination. After coming around one more curve in the creek we saw a frail wooden dock extending outward from the island. The dock pilings consisted of palmetto tree trunks and its flooring and bracing were made with cypress planks. There didn't seem to be much left of the pilings. The marine borers had made them look like hour glasses as you can see from my sketch. The parts of the pilings left seemed to be almost completely covered with barnacles.

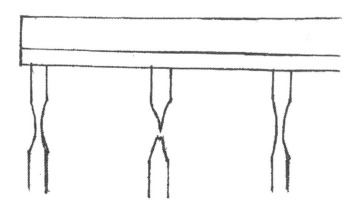

Dock piling damaged by Marine Borers

Dock Piling

We worked our way closer to the dock until we suddenly realized there was a small cabin cruiser anchored on the far side of the dock. We paddled around the dock and up to the cruiser. I was able to tie up to it. As we looked at the vessel Fiona exclaimed in a whisper, "Do you see the name on the side of the boat? It says 'Bobbie's Yacht!' Bobbie must have escaped from Edisto in it and surely must be hiding nearby."

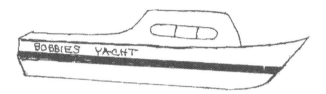

The Mainwaring's cabin boat

Bobbie's Boat

I climbed onto the cruiser and checked to see if anyone was in the cabin, but it was empty. We then pulled over to the dock, tied up to it and gingerly climbed up onto the rickety structure. We almost tiptoed along the dock toward the land as we were afraid the flimsy looking thing might fall down at any moment with the three of us on it.

As we neared the shore we could see tens of thousands of tiny fiddler crabs scurrying along on the mud flats at the upper reaches of the tide. I sketched a male fiddler crab with his large fiddle shaped claw. Fiddler shells are about one inch wide. It is quite amusing to watch the males dashing around, each holding his claw up in the air as though it's a sword ready for combat. In my imagination I can hear them shouting to each other, "En garde!" As a child I used to count how many of them were right handed (that is, right clawed) and how many were left handed. Almost all of them were right handed. I wonder if the left handed ones are considered to be outcasts by the rest of the tribe.

Sand fiddler (its shell is about 1 inch wide)

Fiddler Crab

We reached the end of the dock and looked at the island that was thickly covered with various types of vegetation. There were palmetto trees, water oaks, and great live oak trees with the fascinating Spanish moss hanging down from them. When you look at those old live oak trees with their enormous limbs that may themselves be a few feet in diameter and may extend outward from the tree trunks by 30, 40, 50 or more feet laterally, you will find it hard to understand how they can hold up their own weight without breaking. Some of those limbs look as though they weigh 20 or more tons each.

We started slowly walking into the interior of the island following a recently used path that led into the woods. We were quite cautious as we kept our eyes open for snakes and alligators in the frequent swampy areas along the sides of the path. After we had moved a few hundred yards, we suddenly saw an old gray wooden frame house some distance ahead. At that moment Lt. Seabrook whispered to us to move back down the path a little so we would no longer be visible from the house.

As we moved he said in a very quiet voice, "If someone is hiding here, they may see us coming toward the house and slip out the back to hide somewhere in the forest. Mrs. Mainwaring doesn't know any of us. If she sees a group of strangers coming she will probably be very frightened and run for cover. If that happens we will probably not have sufficient time during this period of high tide to search the entire island for her before we have to leave. The map indicates the island has an area of at least 50 acres. To search an area of land that large, covered in dense almost jungle-like forest, would require a long time. We only have about two hours to stay here. If we stay longer than that we will be stuck here for perhaps an extra ten or eleven hours until the tide comes back in.

"Suppose you two stay right here for five minutes while I slip around through the woods to the back of the house. Then if the two of you will noisily walk up to the front door and knock, I will be in position to catch anyone who may try to escape to the rear."

We followed the plan and after the five minute delay resumed our walk toward the house, talking rather loudly all the way. The exterior of the old house, shaded by several gigantic live oak trees, had certainly seen better days in terms of upkeep. On the front porch were several old rocking chairs and a rusty swing. Just as we started knocking on the front door, we heard sounds of yelling and scuffling from behind the house. In a few moments Lt. Seabrook came around one side of the house almost dragging an attractive but somewhat bedraggled and mosquito bitten young woman who appeared to be in her late twenties.

She was fairly tall, beautifully built, and a vigorous, athletic looking girl. She had jet black hair and lovely brown eyes with long curling eyelashes. Her complexion was as smooth (except where the mosquitoes had been excavating) as the skin of a child. All in all, despite the fact she was dressed in a set of well worn shabby clothes, she was quite a beauty.

Fiona immediately asked, "Are you Bobbie Mainwaring?"

When the young woman tentatively answered in the affirmative, Fiona said, "This is Lt. Seabrook of the Edisto Police Department, and we are Jack and Fiona MacKay. Please don't be alarmed. We are your friends and have been looking for you for several days thinking all the while you have been hiding from someone who must want to kill you. Did you witness the murder of the girl on the beach with that flounder gig?"

After the introductions Bobbie seemed to relax a little and invited us to sit in the chairs on the front porch. She explained, "I had been jogging for about two miles along the beach to the north until I was opposite the first part of the state park near the park's bath house. On that day I was feeling rather lazy and decided to walk up on one of the dunes and rest awhile. By the way, I don't think we are supposed to go up on those dunes as the beach officials are trying to protect and enlarge them.

Anyway, I guess I was fairly well hidden by the pea soup fog, the bushes, the sea oats, and a sand slat fence. I sat there day dreaming for a while when suddenly I was very much alarmed to hear someone near me scream. I looked up just in time to see a black haired girl of just about my size, age, and coloring falling face down near the remains of a sand castle. She had a flounder gig sticking out of her back. As I said, she was quite near me and there was a man behind her who had obviously stuck the gig in her back. The cold shivers in my back really intensified when he said, 'I guess that will shut you up, Bobbie Mainwaring.' He then hastily dragged her over to the sand castle and covered her with sand from the castle walls.

"The visibility in the fog was probably only about 100 feet, and I could see no one else in that limited distance. I quickly ducked down as low as I could and began to crawl face down to the rear of the sand dune expecting a gig in my back at any moment. I was crawling so low to the ground trying to keep out of sight that I was almost underground. I don't think the man ever realized he had been seen, otherwise I'm sure he would immediately have come after me."

In the few minutes she was telling us this information she seemed to relax completely as though a heavy load had been removed from her shoulders, and she apparently had decided to trust us completely. As the worry lines in her face seemed to lessen, I began to realize how lucky John Mainwaring was to have a wife this attractive. In the near future we were to find that she had what I call a bubbling or effervescing personality. Even after her recent frightening adventures she seemed to bubble over with her enthusiasm for living and associating with others.

Bobbie continued her story. "After quickly covering the girl with sand from the castle walls, the man walked away. I lay there on the ground for some time racking my brain trying to figure out what I should do. I knew this killer would soon learn he had killed the wrong person and would come looking for me again."

I could contain myself no longer and asked, "Who was the man?"

When Bobbie replied that she had no idea, I asked, "Couldn't you see him?"

She answered, "Yes, but I couldn't see him very well due to the fog and even more because he was wearing a stocking mask. He, by the way, reminded me of the bank robber I had seen about a year ago at the First Universe Bank where I was working. That man was also wearing a stocking mask that prevented me from seeing his face. I realized that he couldn't be the same person since I had read the newspaper article a few days ago about the first robber confessing to the robbery and dying in the hospital in Columbia. Needless to say, when this second masked man used my name I was frightened out of my skin."

Bobbie continued, "I didn't feel I could return to the Manigault's for fear that my presence there might put them in danger along with me. I sat there behind the sand dune for quite a while trying to figure out some reasonable course of action. Finally, I decided to jog the few blocks over to a house that belongs to some of our friends. The house is located on the back of the island on Jungle Shores Road. I knew they were not in residence at that time. They allow my husband to keep his small cabin cruiser on a tidal creek behind their house. I'm sure you must have seen this boat anchored by the dock as you came onto this island. During the years of our marriage I have often traveled with him on this boat and have learned how to operate it.

"Well, when I arrived at the house, I walked around for a while. No one seemed to be looking so I stepped onto the boat and immediately went into the cabin to put on some of my old fishing clothes I had stored there. We always keep some food, clothes, and plenty of gas on the boat.

"I sat there planning my escape. Finally, the idea came to me to come to this island as almost no one ever comes out here. I waited until the tide was almost fully in and came on over. I knew there were sufficient canned goods stored here in the house to tide me over for quite some time. It was my hope if I stayed here for a few days the police would catch the man who killed the girl on the beach making it safe for me to reappear. Unfortunately, I did not have my cell phone with me to call my husband to tell him where I was hiding."

The house had electricity and water (though with that awful sulfur taste) and a radio. On the boat they had some fishing equipment and a circular shrimp cast net. As Bobbie was a true daughter of coastal South Carolina she could throw the net and catch shrimp and mullet to eat.

My father taught me as a child how to throw a shrimp net. Ever since then I've loved to do it. It's always a thrill to catch some shrimp and also to see the other kinds of sea life you are constantly catching such as crabs and all sorts of fish, usually small. (Here I correct myself somewhat. The crabs are a nuisance as they grab the net with their claws and won't let go.)

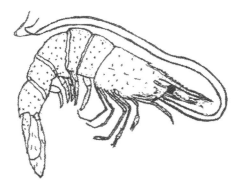

White shrimp that can grow to a length of about 6 inches

Shrimp

During the early summer the shrimp back in the marshes are very small. By the middle of the summer they are still fairly small but are very delicious and sweet to eat. By summer's end and early fall they have reached a very nice edible size. The life of a shrimp is normally about one year. At adulthood the South Carolina ones (white, brown, or pink) are about four to six inches long.

The female carries a clutch of tiny eggs that may number as high as a million. As a result, you might think the ocean would be overflowing with a preponderance of shrimp. Considering the way I like to eat them that abundance would seem rather nice to me. However, crabs, jellyfish and all sorts of other fish love them as much as I do, and they gobble up a large proportion of the larvae as well as the larger shrimp. Then there are the net throwers and the shrimp trawlers that reduce the numbers further.

Individuals with their throw nets catch shrimp toward the end of the summer and on into October. By that time of the year the shrimp are reaching very nice sizes for eating. As we go into October the water temperature begins to cool off, and the shrimp migrate to deeper water. During much of these times the commercial fishermen are catching the shrimp in deep water with their shrimp trawlers and drag nets.

We cast the nets along the shore of the marshes particularly near the entrances of the creeks coming out of the marshes. This is done near low tides as the water has substantially drained from the marshes. At that time the shrimp come out of the marshes and into the deeper water along the shore. As the tide starts coming back in, they move back into the marshes.

As I said the shrimp would be rather small at this time of the summer, but there would be plenty of mullet of good size that Bobbie could catch from the dock at night. If you try to cast a net for mullet during the daytime you probably will not have much luck. Apparently, the mullet see the net or its shadow coming. They are as quick as light and can they jump! As a result, you will probably only catch a few. When it is dark they don't see the net or its shadow. With a few casts you can usually fill a bucket with them. If you cook the mullet immediately after they are caught they are delicious. They don't taste so hot to me a day or two later even though they have been refrigerated.

Another source of food is the easily harvested blue crab, so named for their blue claws. (Actually, their claws are also partly orange in color.) From the middle of spring until the middle of fall they can be caught with baited crab baskets or simply with a piece of twine, a sinker, and a piece of meat. Almost any kind of meat will do such as a piece of fish, but chicken necks are particularly satisfactory.

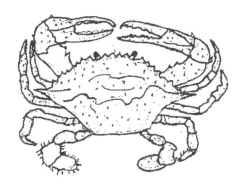

Blue crab with shell as wide as 5 or 6 inches

Blue Crab

The catching of crabs with a piece of meat on a string is much more fun to me than using a crab basket. The line and meat are dropped in the water particularly near the mouths of marsh creeks near low tides. The crabs come along and grab the meat with their claws and are very reluctant to let go. Every once in a while you can slowly pull up the string. The crabs are so dumb they hold onto the meat for dear life. When you get them to the water surface, you dip them out with a dip net and drop them in some type of container such as a basket or large can. If you are crabbing from a small boat, as a rowboat, be sure to wear your shoes. Every once in a while you will drop a crab or two in the boat. You don't want them to get their claws on your pinkies, and they will if you give them half a chance.

By South Carolina law you can only keep crabs that measure five inches or more across the shell from side to side. Should you catch a female with eggs on her abdomen, you need to let her go. A female may be carrying from one to two million eggs at a time. Less than one percent of those larvae will ever reach adulthood at about twelve months of age.

If you have never been out in a motorboat at night with a searchlight near the salt marshes of the Carolina coast, I highly recommend you make such a trip. As you roar along in your boat with your light shining on the water, it is hard to comprehend the amount of sea life you will see, particularly near low tide. The water seems to be alive with myriads of jumping mullet and other fish. I think you will always be glad you made the effort to make such a trip. (By the way, look out for those sand bars. You don't want to run aground as I have done on a few occasions. This is a bad thing to do particularly on a falling tide. You may get stuck and be there for a long time.)

Fiona questioned Bobbie, "What have you done to help pass the time since you arrived on this island?"

"Well, it has been quiet and lonely. I didn't know what to do other than jog, sunbathe, read, fish, and try to think of some course of action. I've listened to the radio news hoping to hear the killer had been arrested but that never happened. My biggest worry has been the fear my husband must have concerning my whereabouts. I was hoping he would eventually guess where I was when he discovered his boat was missing."

Lt. Seabrook spoke up, "We have to make some quick decisions because we have less than one hour before the tide is too low for us to leave. Mrs. Mainwaring, do you want to return to Edisto with us today?"

Tensing up, Bobbie replied, "I would love to be back on Edisto. But, as strange as this may sound, I feel safer here. I am terrified of being recognized by that killer. At the same time I miss my husband and don't want him to continue to worry. I just don't know what to do."

"I have a thought that may help," I volunteered. "The three of us could return to Edisto today and leave Bobbie here. She has managed well and will do fine for two more nights. If the killer has not been apprehended in the next day or so, Fiona will go to the Manigault home carrying a large shopping bag filled with newspapers. After paying a short visit, she will leave with her shopping bag stuffed with some of Bobbie's clothes and other personal possessions. We'll bring those clothes when we return to this island on Monday."

Fiona nodded, "We will also bring some items to alter your appearance. I like to think I'm pretty good at creating disguises for people in hiding, and I love the challenge."

"That's correct. She loves any challenge. So in two days Lt. Seabrook, Fiona and I will come back to this island with the plan of taking a disguised Bobbie back to Edisto and have her move in with us. How does that sound, Bobbie?"

"It sounds good. But my big concern is still my husband. I know he is worried and I really want to get in touch with him and assure him that I am OK."

"That's not a problem," I tried to calm her. "We will tell John that you are alive but now have bleached hair and some other changes to your appearance. We'll explain that temporarily you are living with us. You'll be safer with us and not returning to your Charleston home since the killer may be closely watching your home and your husband in an effort to find you. We will ask John not to visit us for fear someone might be following him. We could, however, arrange for him to accidentally meet you on the beach one day next week.

"At that time we can introduce him to my cousin Rachel Golightly of Beaufort, South Carolina who is staying with us for a while. I will instruct John beforehand to briefly shake hands with her and then after a minute or two to continue his walk. We want him to be assured that his Bobbie is alive and well."

Bobbie spoke up and said, "If my hair is blonde he might be rather upset. When I was a teenager I always wanted to bleach my hair, but when I mentioned it to my mother, she would almost go into apoplexy and mumble something about her only daughter becoming a woman of the street."

We assured Bobbie that we would warn her husband in advance of any changes that had been made in her appearance.

I asked the lieutenant, "What do you think of this plan? Does it sound safe to you?"

"I think it will be OK, but we'll still have to be on the look out for anything suspicious. Now time is passing and we have to be on the move soon."

Fiona gave Bobby the fresh food we had brought as well as some books, newspapers, and the insect repellant. She was absolutely elated to receive the repellant. I then went back to the runabout and brought up the lunch Mrs. Seabrook had prepared for us. Bobbie apparently hadn't been eating too well as she really dug into the delicious food. We then had to leave the island. Bobbie hugged us all, and we assured her we would be back on Monday with the items for her disguise. We told her we would return her to Edisto once her disguise was complete.

On Monday it would be my duty to take the cabin cruiser back to the house on Jungle Shores Road. Once there I could easily walk back to our rental house. Fiona could drive herself and Bobbie back to our rental house.

Chapter Twelve

Bobbie Returns to Edisto

igh tide on Monday at Mainwaring Island was roughly 1:00 in the afternoon. About an hour before that time the three of us arrived at the island. Bobbie was sitting on the dock happily anticipating her trip back to civilization. The first item of business was to work on Bobbie's disguise. Since shopping at Edisto is limited, Fiona had visited the local Piggly Wiggly to purchase a package of hair dye, or as the package read "colorant." When the girls took off to play beauty shop, I read the box. Interesting! "Extra Light Natural Blonde, Rich Luminous Conditioning, From Paris." I guess they can charge more if they tell consumers it's from Paris.

When Fiona and Bobbie emerged from their "beauty shop," I was astounded. The results were amazing! Maybe those Parisians really do know what to do with hair.

I spoke to the blonde beauty with Fiona, "Hello, Rachel Golightly."

She smiled, "I think 'Prudence' sounds better than 'Rachel.'"

I grinned. "Hello, Prudence Golightly. You know those names 'Prudence' and 'Golightly' do go well together. They both mean about the same thing."

Admiring Bobbie's hair, Fiona said, "Isn't it amazing what can come out of a bottle. Your hair looks so good I might bleach my own curly locks."

Bobbie was alarmed. "Oh no! Your red hair is so beautiful you must never change it." Then she laughingly continued, "Furthermore, you don't want to join me and those other women out on the street do you?"

As the tide was just about at its highest point, Fiona, Prudence, and Lt. Seabrook stepped into his runabout and started the trip back to Edisto. I waited about 15 minutes and then followed in the little cabin boat.

After proceeding out of the marsh and across the river, I anchored the boat at the house on Jungle Shores Road and walked to our place. Fiona and Prudence were already there.

Soon after breakfast the next morning I drove to the Holy City to the law firm on Meeting Street where John Mainwaring practiced. My purpose was to tell him of the whereabouts of his wife and to assure him of her well being.

Without an appointment I walked into the law offices and spoke to the receptionist. When I told her I would like to see Mr. Mainwaring although I did not have an appointment, she said she could arrange one later in the week. I told her I had a bit of information of considerable interest to Mr. Mainwaring and needed to see him right then for only a few minutes. She informed me that would not be possible. We argued back and forth for a while.

Finally, I asked her if she could keep a secret. Upon her assurance that she could, I said I would like to give Mr. Mainwaring some information of great importance. If she would work me into his schedule for just a few minutes and he was not pleased that she had done so, I would give her $100 in cash on the spot.

This offer seemed to inspire her as she hopped right up and went into the lawyer's office. She returned almost immediately to say he would see me in about five minutes. True to his word, I was soon ushered in to see him. He was a fairly tall, erect, man with blonde hair who looked as though he had not slept lately. I introduced myself and told him that while my wife and I were vacationing at Edisto Beach we had come across some information of immense interest to him. He seemed rather suspicious of me until I told him I had seen his diplomas on the wall and realized we were fellow alumni of The Citadel. From then on he warmed up considerably and listened very carefully to my words.

I told him a little of how my wife and I had participated in the solution of several murder mysteries in the past and then of our discovery of the girl's body on Edisto Beach a few days before. I went on to tell him how the Edisto police had given us permission to work on the case. I said we knew of their initial identification of the girl as his wife, and we knew of his wife's disappearance. I then told him we had found Bobbie. Up until this point he had seemed only slightly interested in my spiel. But when I said we had found his wife, he jumped out of his chair shouting, "Is she all right? Where is she?"

I told him she was staying with us at Edisto and was quite well although rather sunburned and mosquito bitten. He sat back in his chair with a smile on his face. At about that time his receptionist came rushing into his office asking if he was all right. She said she had heard him shouting. When she saw him smiling all over, she apologized for her intrusion and quickly left the office with a frown on her face. Perhaps she knew she had just lost $100.

I told John that Bobbie had seen the killer of the girl on the beach but could not recognize him since it was extremely foggy that morning and he was wearing a stocking mask. Further I said she heard the killer say, "I guess that will shut you up, Bobbie Mainwaring." Upon hearing these words, John visibly shuddered and said, "Oh, my poor little darling."

I continued telling him that Bobbie thought it would be wise to go into hiding since she knew the killer would soon discover he had killed the wrong girl and would in all probability come looking for her again. I also described how Bobbie, after much thought, decided to jog over to the Edisto Marina and take his cabin boat to Mainwaring Island.

At this point John asked, "Why didn't I think of the possibility of her taking the boat? I have not even thought of going by Jungle Shores Road to check it since Bobbie disappeared."

I told John the murderer apparently thinks Bobbie can identify him as the second robber at the First Universe Bank, but Bobbie has no idea as to the man's identity. I told John how we had brought Bobbie back to Edisto the day before and how we were keeping her in our rented house. I explained we had altered her appearance quite a bit by changing her hair color. John again shuddered and expressed some alarm at the idea of changing her lovely black hair. When he made his comment I told him Bobbie's story about wanting to be blonde when she was a teen and how her mother had a fit and put her foot down as she mumbled something about her little daughter becoming a woman of the street.

I went on to say, "When Bobbie goes out of the house she will be wearing large dark glasses and will have a few bandages on her arms and legs. She will claim to anyone who asks that she was in a recent automobile wreck." I also told him we were passing her off as a cousin of mine, Prudence Golightly from Beaufort, S. C. When he heard this name, John laughed out loud.

John asked if he could return with me to Edisto so he could see her. I explained, "We have no idea who the man is who tried to kill her. Thus we cannot risk leading him to Prudence if he happens to be following you. I think that is a very strong possibility because I bet he may very well think you know where she is hiding. However, if you will come walking down the beach at Edisto at a time we mutually agree on, you will accidentally encounter us, and I will introduce you to Prudence."

To conclude our conversation we agreed that he would go to Edisto at 11:00 the next morning and walk down the beach to the south and past our block of Palmetto Boulevard. Along there he would see us up on the beach sunbathing. I told him to look for me or for my wife with her flaming red hair that a person could spot at a distance of several hundred yards. "When you come over to meet us remember there should be no hugging, kissing, or lengthy hand holding. We do not know if someone will be following you in hopes that you will lead him to Bobbie. We will have Bobbie looking carefully at everyone near you on the beach to see if she recognizes someone who might have been involved in some way with the bank."

I soon left the office and a very happy John Mainwaring. As I walked through the outer office I thanked the receptionist for working me into John's schedule. "Sorry you don't get the $100 because your boss seemed delighted to talk to me just as I told you he would. However, here is half the prize for you to buy yourself a couple of lunches."

She thanked me and asked what kind of profession I was in.

My answer was, "Don't you recognize an old fogey college professor when you see one?"

Just after 10:30 the next morning Fiona, Prudence, and I walked down to the beach to sit on our beach towels and soak up a little sunshine. At a few minutes past 11:00 John came strolling down the beach. Edisto is not a crowded place and there were only 10 or 15 people in our general area. As a result, he had no difficulty spotting us. He first saw Fiona's hair and then me. He veered over in our direction and loudly exclaimed, "Hello, Jack MacKay." Though he spoke to me he had eyes only for the blonde-headed Prudence and vice versa.

After I responded to his greeting I introduced him to Fiona and Prudence. He expressed great pleasure in meeting my wife and cousin. He commented to Prudence, "You have such a wonderful name."

Prudence asked me, "Are all your male friends as attractive as this one?"

I quietly interrupted and said, "Prudence, don't stare at John. You are supposed to be looking at the people walking on the beach to see if you recognize someone following John."

John continued very quietly, "Oh, Prudie, I've missed you so much. By the way, your hair is beautiful. All in all, you are the loveliest girl in the world, and this is the happiest day of my life!"

Prudence replied, "I have also missed you terribly, but since we bleached my hair I have been rather frightened for you to see me. I was afraid you might disown me when you saw my hair."

John replied that he had always wondered how it would be to have a blonde wife and he loved it. As he looked at her bandages, he said, "Have you been fighting and come out second best?"

She replied that she had been in an altercation but he should see the other girl. After a few more pleasant comments were exchanged we told John he had better leave. We suggested it would be best for him not to frequent this area of the beach until the killer was apprehended. We hoped that would be fairly soon but we couldn't promise anything. John then walked on down the beach and came back past us about 20 minutes later waving to us as he passed.

Chapter Thirteen

A Frightening Idea

W e talked with Bobbie on so many occasions about the day of the robberies and questioned her so much about the second robbery in particular that she said she felt as though we were conducting a Spanish Inquisition with her as the inquisitee. We particularly wanted to know if she knew anything about the second robbery. How did that robber know her name? She was very puzzled over that also, but she did tell us she had a name plate on her desk in the lobby. We asked her if it were possible for one of her fellow employees to have taken the money and sneaked it out of the bank without getting caught.

She replied, "Perhaps one of the employees could have pocketed a few hundred dollars and safely escaped with it but there seems to me to be no way he or she could have taken $490,000 without being observed by several coworkers. I admit that the police didn't seem to pay much attention to what we, the bank employees, were doing in the aftermath of the first robbery. I'm certain their thoughts were that the robbery was a past event and their efforts were directed at catching its perpetrator. Surely they had no idea a second robbery was taking place right under their noses or was about to take place."

"Well, here is another thought we had," I continued. "Do you think it would it be practical for someone to put money in a garbage bag and dump it into a trash can? Doing this would necessitate an evening visit by the robber to the dumpster behind the bank to retrieve the bag."

Bobbie thought about this. "I'm pretty sure that would not have worked because the police checks included the trash. But remember I did not return to the bank that night so I didn't see any diving activity at the dumpster."

Now it was Fiona's turn to question. "Do you think anyone could have shipped the money out in the mail or with FedEx or UPS?"

Bobbie gave the same answer. "I'm quite sure a plan like that wouldn't work. No one could have mailed a significant sum of money by US Mail, FedEx or UPS because the bank had a policy requiring a detailed check of the contents of packages by more than one person before any packages could be sealed and sent. I can tell the two of you have given this problem a lot of thought. Keep it up and maybe soon you will hit the right answer."

Soon after supper that evening Fiona walked out onto the front porch where she sat in one of the rocking chairs and began to vigorously rock. This she continued to do for such a long time that Bobbie asked me if she was all right.

I whispered to her, "Don't say anything. Fiona loves to rock when she has some deep thinking she wants to do about some problem and, boy, is she good at solving problems."

Well finally, after a long period of continuous rocking and deep thinking, Fiona said to us, "We need to talk about the different groups of people and the individuals who might have been involved in committing these crimes."

She then proceeded to list groups and individuals who might have been involved. These were:

1. the bank employees
2. the bank customers
3. the first robber
4. some other person or persons

Fiona continued, "Now if we examine each of these groups or individuals we can make the following statements concerning them and perhaps rule out several of them.

"First, Bobbie has told us the second robber and the man who tried to kill her probably could not have been one of the bank employees because they would have had so much difficulty stealing the money unobserved and getting it out of the bank.

"Second, bank customers could not possibly wander freely around the area where the tellers work or in the bank vault. If they had done so they would have been seen immediately and told to leave. This would have been particularly true after the first robbery when everyone was alert, and the police were everywhere. If these customers had started picking up $20 and $100 bills and stuffing them in their pockets, they would have been buried beneath the jail before dark. Thus, I think we can rule them out of possible consideration.

"Third, the first robber did not return to the bank that day. In fact in his deathbed confession he said he got his $110,000, cleared out of Charleston immediately, and never returned. So he is out of it.

"Fourth, this seems to leave us with only one group of people who could wander at will around the bank and who could pick up the money, examine it, and perhaps pocket it. After I reveal the name of this group, the mayor of Charleston will surely decline to give us a key to his city. On the other hand, we may be given free room and board at the city jail or perhaps be sent on an involuntary vacation voyage in the Hunley submarine to the bottom of the sea. This group consists of the six city policemen who were sent to the bank after the first robbery. At the moment, it seems to me they are the only ones who could have gotten the money out of the bank on that day—but $490,000? It may have seemed to this officer or officers that there was little danger if they took advantage of the situation and stole some of the bank's money. It would probably be thought that all of the missing money was taken by the first robber. But then on his deathbed Mr. Musgrove unwittingly threw a monkey wrench into the idea that the second robbery would remain undiscovered when he revealed the amount of money he had taken."

I tried to sum it all up. "For some reason this new robber or robbers thought Bobbie could identify him or them. As a result, an effort was made to eliminate her but the wrong girl, Martha Ulmer, was killed. Perhaps this shows the man trying to kill Bobbie only had a general idea as to what she looked like."

We all thought Fiona's speculation that one or more of the members of Charleston's finest were guilty of robbery was not going to be popular with that group. We were going to have to keep a low profile any time we returned to visit the city. How was I going to ever go to another of the Friday afternoon parades at The Citadel without constantly looking over my shoulder to see if I was going to be arrested for loitering, parking in an illegal spot, disorderly conduct, or some other dreamed up law violation? But what other possibility was there?

Fiona simply voiced the opinion that one or more of the city's officers could be rotten and had been planning this kind of robbery for some time. She thought he or they might have had the idea to do this from the first time they were assigned to be part of a team sent to investigate a bank robbery. In other words, maybe they thought if additional money was sneaked out of a bank just after an armed robbery, everyone would think all the missing money was taken during the first robbery. They may have waited for months for an armed robbery to occur and then pounced. When we asked Bobbie if she thought it was feasible for one or more of the officers to take the money, she said she thought it was possible for them to slip out a few thousand dollars but never could they have gotten away with $490,000.

The next morning we got Bobbie to walk down to the beach and take a sunbath in an area where there were quite a few other people around. We asked her to stay there while we went to the police station to see Lt. Seabrook. Once at the station we told him of Fiona's conclusion as to the group she thought had an opportunity to take the money and get away with it. To our amazement, he didn't seem to be surprised by our conclusions. I think he had probably been thinking along the same lines. As a matter of fact, he seemed rather sad as he listened to our conclusions and somewhat reluctantly nodded his head in agreement. After sitting quietly and thinking with his head in his hands, he said he was going to have to pass these ideas on to the Charleston police. In a rather woebegone manner he told us of his previous good relations with the Charleston police department and expressed his fears that those good relations might be coming to a sudden end on this day.

Chapter Fourteen

Headed to Jail

Fiona, Lt. Seabrook, and I drove from Edisto Beach inland to US Highway 17, the Ocean Highway, and then on up to Charleston. The highway runs from the southwest to the northeast right across the peninsula where the central part of the city is located. We crossed the Ashley River Bridge and rode onto the peninsula. We turned left or to the north and headed toward that marvelous college (The Citadel, of course). We soon came to the police station on Lockwood Avenue quite near The Citadel football field at Johnson Hagood Stadium.

Tom was taking us to see a Captain La Roche who was the officer in charge of the six policemen who had been sent to the First Universe Bank on the day of the armed robbery last year. All three of us were quite apprehensive of the reception the captain would give us when we expressed the opinion that one or more of his men might very well have been involved in the second robbery.

As we walked from the car toward the front door of the station, Tom Seabrook jokingly asked if we had brought with us some toothbrushes, tubes of toothpaste, and a pair or two of pajamas in case we were invited to stay for a little while as special guests of the Charleston Police Department.

Fiona responded, "They may think you are the one who needs rest and relaxation the most of the three of us. If that should be the case would you like us to take your police car back to Edisto and park in front or your home or at the Edisto Police Station?"

He smiled weakly at her question. "I guess the station would be the best place to leave it."

Captain La Roche, who was born on nearby Johns Island, was a heavy set, rugged looking individual with a determined looking chin and piercing blue eyes. He was definitely a man whose side I would like to be on in case there was a brawl. Despite his appearance, he had a delightful smile and spoke with that wonderful lilting Charleston accent. (I still consider it the most attractive accent you will hear wherever you may go.)

After Tom Seabrook had introduced us to the captain and told him of our voluntary work on the sand castle murder, he said, "George, we have been friends for a long time, and I hope that will still be the case after this meeting is over. We are going to tell you about an idea we have had concerning one or more of your officers and their relation to the second robbery at the First Universe Bank as well as the recent murder on the beach at Edisto. I know you don't want to hear it, but I feel we must pass it on to you."

The captain smiled, perhaps a little sadly, "I thought all three of you looked a little worried when you trooped into my office. But, Tom, I think we will always be friends whatever unpleasant tasks may come our way in this police world. So let's have it. Tell me what this new trouble is that we are going to have to face together."

Tom thanked the captain and said he would like Fiona to present her deductions regarding the robberies and the murder at Edisto. She described the first three possibilities for the identity of the second bank robber and told how she felt each of those possibilities didn't seem feasible to her. After she presented the fourth possibility, Captain La Roche moaned, "Oh, me. This is going to be a bad day, but, Tom, our friendship still stands. Mrs. MacKay, you are telling me about a thought that has been running around the periphery of my brain for the last few days. However, I just have not let myself believe it. Surely such a situation could not occur here in the Charleston Police Department. I just have not been willing to face the facts you have so clearly presented to me. I've tried so hard to push any thought that we could possibly have one or more rotten eggs in what I think is our wonderful department."

Fiona spoke up, "I'm not saying the robber and murderer was a Charleston policeman. Rather, I am saying from the information we now have, those men were in a position where they could have stolen some of the money. In other words, we have no evidence to show the police were involved in any way in the crimes, but we have no evidence to show they were not involved. As a result, I think this is a possibility that should be investigated. To be truthful, however, I can see they were in a position where they could have stolen some of the money, but I don't see any way they could have taken $490,000. I really don't see how anyone else could have taken that much money right under the noses of the police and the various bank employees."

The captain responded, "I understand what you are saying, Mrs. MacKay. All we can do is face the facts and see if we can discover the identity of the scoundrel or scoundrels who committed these crimes. When we do, and if we find he is one of my own men, you may have to restrain me from forcing him to join the twenty-nine pirates who from time to time can supposedly still be seen hanging from the infamous live oak trees at the Battery."

We then told Captain La Roche how Bobbie Mainwaring had gone into hiding after the beach murder fearing the killer would soon be coming after her. We also related how we had found her and brought her back to Edisto to our rented house. I asked the captain if there was some way we could have videos made of each of the six officers who went to the bank on that fatal day. My purpose was to show them to Bobbie to see if she could make an identification. In addition, I thought if she heard the voices and saw the pictures of the men at the same time, she might be able to say that one particular officer reminded her of the killer for whom we were searching.

The captain said he would have each of the six men read a paragraph or two from *The Post and Courier* and video their readings. He said he would tell the men the department was planning to prepare a documentary on Charleston law enforcement (a true statement) and various participants from the department would be needed. Thus, these recorded readings would help the department select the officers with the best voices.

When we stood up to leave, the captain laughed and said to us, "If you brought toothbrushes and extra clothing anticipating you might be staying with us for a while, you can breathe a little easier now as you will not need them—at least not on this day."

We returned to Edisto and walked down to the beach to find Bobbie. There we found a lonely looking girl. However, she immediately perked up when she saw us. She had spent her day alone reading and sitting in the sunshine apparently dreaming of going home to Charleston. Normally I think such a day would have been delightful to her, but perhaps not when she had to sit there worrying about every man she saw on the beach, wondering if one of them could be the one who had tried to gig her on that foggy morning.

True to the captain's words, videos of the six officers on whom we had cast suspicion were brought to us the next day by a Sergeant Maybank. Each of the men was shown reading a section of *The Post and Courier*. The sergeant showed the videos to Bobbie several times and interviewed her in detail as to her recent experiences. Unfortunately, Bobbie could not identify any of the men as a possibility nor could she say a single one of the voices was in any way familiar to her. She did say she had the impression one of the policemen seemed much taller than the killer and another one much shorter. Sergeant Maybank carefully recorded her remarks and headed back to the Holy City.

Chapter Fifteen

Is the Money Still in the Bank?

During the next few days after our visit with Captain La Roche, he conducted an extremely thorough undercover investigation of the financial condition of the six officers who had been sent to the First Universe Bank on the day of the robbery-murder. He was able to obtain court orders for these investigations after he explained the items he wanted to look into and what he expected to learn.

The men were questioned in great detail. They were checked for major changes in their financial situation including their ownership of stocks and bonds. Also looked for were sudden increases in ownership of land, gold and silver coins, rare stamps, and so on.

The only suspicious item discovered was a sudden increase in one of the officer's bank accounts. The increase of over $200,000 had occurred very shortly after the bank robberies and the murder of the teller. The situation aroused much suspicion among the investigating officers. However, when the matter was investigated in detail it was discovered that the money had been left to him by an aunt who had recently passed away at her home in Augusta, Georgia. Captain La Roche, himself, drove over to Augusta to check the accuracy of the report. The inheritance was confirmed, and he returned to Charleston in a far better humor than when he left because it seemed none of his men were involved in the crime.

Even though the captain thought all of his men were now in the clear, he nevertheless arranged a lineup of the six officers for Bobbie to observe. We secretly took her to the Charleston police station one day. There the six men were required to come out one at a time wearing a stocking mask and say a few sentences. The last sentence spoken quite loudly by each man was, "I guess that will shut you up, Bobbie Mainwaring."

After seeing all the men, Bobbie confessed not one of them reminded her in any way of the man who killed the girl on the beach. Furthermore, she felt not one of the men seemed hesitant to speak as they might very well have been if they had been guilty of the crime.

Shortly after these investigations were completed, we again visited Captain La Roche. He now looked much less worried than when we had last seen him. He obviously was elated over the fact that all of his men had been cleared of any complicity in the second robbery and the murder at Edisto Beach. In fact he said to us, "I'm quite pleased we have been unable to find any evidence of wrongdoing by my men in this case."

He then asked, "Do you have any other ideas as to how the money could have been removed from the bank?"

I answered his question, "There seem to be no carrier pigeons around who could have carried out the money, and flushing the money down the commode seems very impractical. To me, therefore, if the money was taken out of the bank there seems to be only one other way it could have been done—with the body of the dead teller. But that really does not seem to be very practical to me. One trouble with this idea is the people working with the body were not free to wander around the bank and pick up stacks of bills, carry them over to the body, and stuff them into the clothes of the dead man."

The captain agreed with me that the possibility of the money having been removed with the dead teller seemed very remote, but he would nevertheless look into it. He said, "I confess we have not checked this possibility very carefully, and that is my fault. I know the county medical examiner and the coroner very well. I would trust my life to either one of them. I cannot believe either of them would steal the bank's money no matter how much was available. It is possible, however, that they were used unknowingly by someone else who in some way stashed the money with the body. I will have that possibility looked into carefully. But what did you mean when you said 'if' the money had been taken out?"

I explained, "I don't believe the money was taken out with the body. In fact, I am beginning to think it was not taken out of the bank at all on that day. I believe it was hidden somewhere in the bank and is probably still there."

Captain La Roche said, "You may be right and I will have the bank searched again, this time with tremendous care. On our first trip to the bank we didn't really look for hidden money because we had no idea there had been a second robbery."

The president of the bank, Mr. Rivers, signed a consent form to allow the detectives to search the bank again. As a result, a search warrant was not necessary. The bank was searched from top to bottom with a fine tooth comb by several very competent detectives. They painstakingly searched all the desks, floor drains, clocks, stuffing in the chairs and sofas, water fountains, behind the wall pictures, the tennis racquet cases, the refrigerator, behind the electrical outlets, in the ducts, and everything else they could think of. They even checked every piece of floor tile to see if any were loose and would come up to reveal a hiding place. They made similar checks of the walls and ceiling. Unfortunately, no hiding places and no money were found. Can you think of any place they missed?

Fiona and I were allowed to participate in this search. In a storage room on the second floor we found several hundred pink ceramic piggy banks. They ranged in size from small (three inches high) to large (15 inches high). These banks were given to children coming into First Universe Bank with their parents with the hope the gift would encourage them to develop the habit of saving.

When we found there was a large cork stopper in the bottom of each pig providing access to its contents, we were quite excited thinking we might find the missing money therein.

We laboriously removed the stoppers from every one of those pigs. Surprisingly, each pig contained some money, but it was only seed money—a quarter, a dime, a nickel, and a penny.

The detectives also looked into the removal of the teller's body on the day of the robberies and murder. On that day soon after the police arrived, a medical technician and the coroner had arrived and checked to see if the teller was still alive, but that was not the case. The medical technician remained with the body until it was removed from the bank. He had not wandered around the bank where he might have been able to pick up a few bills.

In Charleston the coroner at the time of the robberies was a female nurse who had the duty of investigating natural deaths caused by traffic accidents, suicides, drug overdoses, and shootings. Her work also included efforts to identify the dead as well as the notification of relatives after identifications had been made. In my opinion, she surely had a difficult job. I have been told that the medical examiner's office in Charleston has recently been closed, but the county of Charleston does still have a medical examiner. The body of the teller was taken to the morgue and put in one of those trays where it was kept until instructions were received from the police. In this case the man's death was clearly caused by a gunshot, and the autopsy was just a legal formality.

Chapter Sixteen

Why is the Killer after Bobbie?

We were at a dead standstill in this investigation. We had run into the proverbial brick wall. No one had been able to discover how the second robbery had been committed nor where the money was hidden. The police seemed to think, as Fiona and I did, the money was still hidden at the bank.

What else could the police do? They decided to keep searching the bank but now they brought in different searchers. First they asked SLED (South Carolina Law Enforcement Division) to search the building. This excellent group, proud of their reputation, searched the building for an entire day and declared no money was hidden there.

The FBI had been working on this case all along so Captain La Roche asked them if they would conduct a search. They did but with the same results as the other groups. Mr. Rivers, beginning to show some signs of exasperation, once again permitted these latter searches so search warrants were not required.

After these unsuccessful searches, Captain La Roche vowed, "We are going to find that money if we have to tear that bank down brick by brick and then split each of the bricks wide open."

Fiona and I had not been invited to be on hand for these latter searches, and I don't think we could have helped even if we had been there. After those last two groups reported they had found nothing, I was almost ready to throw my hands up in dismay and go back to our home in Bonnie Glen. We had two more weeks before our long vacation was over, and we didn't seem to have a clue as to the identity of the second robber-murderer. We didn't know whether he hid the money in the bank or took it out in some miraculous way. Everything we had suggested or looked into had come to nothing.

It was at this point I injected another possibility as to what had happened to the money. I theorized, "If I had worked for the bank, taken the money and hidden it somewhere in the building, what would I do next? The answer is once every day or two I would go to my hidden money and put a handful of it in my pocket then take it with me when I left the bank. If I followed that procedure for a few months or even for a year without getting caught, I would have in all probability cleaned out all the money. Even if I had been caught with a pocketful of money I would have claimed it was mine. If a check were made of the bank's money at that time, no new loss would be discovered. If this is what occurred we may never discover what happened to the money or who took it."

Fiona did not agree with my idea because she thought if that had happened, the police in their investigations of the employees of the bank would, in all probability, have discovered a significant change in the financial status of one of them. She further said if the money had been taken out as I suggested, the thief would have had to find some other place to hide it. What better place could he have found than the one where he hid it since no one else could find it?

"Maybe," I said partly in jest, "the second thief dug a hole in one of the concrete floors or walls and buried the money there. Or maybe there never was a second robbery."

Fiona replied, "Your suggestions cannot be correct. Someone took the money and hid it very well. If no one took it or if it was hidden in the bank and all of it removed, why did someone try to kill Bobbie who worked in the bank at the time of the robberies? We are just going to have to come up with another approach. I think the most suggestive thing that has happened is the fact that the killer wants to find and eliminate Bobbie. What could she know that the other bank employees do not? It is my belief the second robber thinks Bobbie saw or heard something he knows will convict him if it is revealed. However, Bobbie seems to have no idea what it might be. In other words, she may have heard or seen some incriminating things, but she doesn't have any idea what those things may be."

She continued, "Bobbie may have seen something the robber realizes may sink his ship if it is revealed. We are going to have to keep after her night and day picking her brain as to her experiences at the bank. This will include the things she saw and heard on that fateful day and since that day last year. We must get her to tell us things that happened to her or things she witnessed when she worked at the bank, even the things that may sound trivial.

"We have eliminated all the bank employees, the police, the undertaker, the bank customers, and everyone else we could imagine from participating in the crime. This just can't be correct. Someone in one of these groups has outsmarted us and is just laughing at us right now."

Fiona suggested to Captain La Roche that there was one thing the police had not done—check the five male bank employees with the same detail they had used to check their own officers who had descended on the bank immediately after the bank killing and first robbery.

She told him, "By process of elimination I now think one of the male bank employees must be guilty."

My comment to Fiona was, "If this investigation of the male bank employees proves fruitless, I will believe there was no second robbery, and Mr. Musgrove and the bank examiner can't count."

Captain La Roche, agreeing with Fiona and not me, immediately launched another detailed investigation of the five male bank employees. This investigation, as for the six policemen, involved their financial activities including large purchases and investments, girlfriends, lavish vacations, gambling, safe deposit boxes, detailed searches of their homes, and so on and so on. Several days were required to conduct this latest search. The police even followed the five men when they were away from the bank to see what they did in their free time.

The net result of all these activities was nothing useful. Determined to solve these crimes, Fiona and I resumed our questioning of Bobbie about that bad day at the bank a year ago. We went over and over the events of that day so many times Bobbie was nearly in tears. Finally, I had what was rare for me––a bright idea.

I said, "We have questioned poor Bobbie so many times with no results that I believe she saw nothing of significance on that day. I think the second robbery occurred on the day of the first robbery and murder, but I think the incriminating thing Bobbie saw perhaps occurred at some other time before the robbery. The robber-murderer believes if she ever thinks back to that observation it will point directly at him as the guilty person. He must think some day she will remember what she saw him do or say."

Bobbie moaned, "Oh, me. Does this mean you are going to have another inquisition covering my every day at the bank over the two year period I worked for them? If so, we may be here for years, and I'll never get to go home again. By the time I do, John may have a new girlfriend."

Fiona remarked, "Every once in a blue moon Jack comes up with a good idea. You remember the old saying, 'Even a blind hog finds an acorn now and then.' This saying certainly applies to Jack on this occasion. His idea is, I think, a super one and it will not be as tough on you as you may think. I would like to suggest we give you five little notebooks. Then please put the name of one of the bank's five male employees on each one. Please start making notes in these books of your conversations and associations with these men. Try to remember every meeting and conversation you ever had with each of them no matter how trivial it may seem and include your observations of things you may have seen them doing, no matter how innocent they may have seemed to you at the time.

"Review your lists several times spending all of today and however long it takes. Then go over your notes with Jack and me telling us about the men's habits, what they did for lunch, hobbies they may have, what they did on coffee breaks, how they went about their jobs, what they said they did on their weekends, and so on. Bobbie, remember we are not having this interrogation for fun, although it is fun having you with us. Your very life is in danger."

With a very solemn face, Bobbie nodded in agreement.

Over the next two days we followed this lead and talked and questioned Bobbie hour after hour. The result of all our work seemed to be nothing. However, we asked Bobbie to keep going over the lists and adding to them.

At the end of the second day we decided to have a break and rent a tennis court at the resort on the back of the island for a couple of hours. We had by now discarded Bobbie's bandages. The three of us hit balls for a while until a young man came up and asked if he could play with us. We played a couple of interesting sets. There was one strange thing though, and that was something Bobbie did. I would often see her between points looking at her tennis racquet as though she was bewildered about something. But she seemed unable to figure out what it was.

After tennis Bobbie told us she wanted to have a further vacation from the questioning for the rest of the day. When we agreed, she said she was going to fix "Frogmore Stew" for our evening meal. This stew is a very simple one to prepare but it is extremely popular in South Carolina, particularly among beach goers. The origin of Frogmore Stew, which contains no frogs, is open to some dispute. In South Carolina its origin is usually credited to a man named Richard Gay, who lived in a small town named Frogmore, near Beaufort, South Carolina not far from Edisto as the crow flies. If Mr. Gay is the person who originally developed this marvelous dish, I think he deserves no less than a Nobel Prize for Gastronomic Delights.

The ingredients in the stew include roughly the following: one half pound of shrimp per person, several ears of corn cut into quarters, one half pound of Kielbasa sausage per person, new unpeeled red potatoes, some vinegar and some seafood seasoning. To cook the stew, water is placed in a large pot and about one-half cup of vinegar is added along with various seasonings. The water is heated until it boils. Then the potatoes are tossed in and cooked for about ten or 15 minutes. Then the sausage links are added and cooked until the water again returns to a boil in five or so minutes. The corn is next added and cooked for about five minutes. Finally, the shrimp are added and cooked for five or six minutes, or until they turn pink.

About the only thing you have to be careful about is overcooking the shrimp. When the shrimp are done, the water is drained from the stew, and the stew is ready for serving. Some people serve the stew by pouring it out onto newspapers covering the table. Cocktail sauce is provided for the shrimp and the sausage. You are now ready for a treat!

Along with our stew Bobbie and I enjoyed a couple of glasses of beer. Fiona, however, does not really care for alcoholic beverages other than an occasional glass of wine. She jokingly gave us a lecture on the evils of demon rum, particularly beer guzzling. In response we told her the water she was drinking despite its treatment contained bacteria while the beer we were drinking had none since it had gone through a treatment process of filtration, boiling, and so on. Then I repeated some words supposedly said by Ben Franklin on this subject:

In wine there is wisdom.
In beer there is freedom.
In water there is bacteria.

Fiona, ignoring our comments, went along drinking the water from the fire station while Bobbie and I, ignoring Fiona's advice, continued enjoying our beer. I reminded Fiona that my doctor had suggested I drink a glass or two of wine each day or a glass or two of beer. Fiona told me one glass of wine or one glass of beer each day was sufficient. Furthermore, she said she was sure the doctor was not thinking I would use twenty ounce glasses. She was sure he was referring to a five ounce glass of wine or a twelve ounce can of beer.

As we sat there after dinner I said to Bobbie, "Why did you leave your bank job so shortly after the day of the robberies and murder of the teller?"

Bobbie laughingly replied, "Do you think I rushed out with a great big bag of money? I didn't really want to leave as I was very fond of my job and the people I worked with. But after the robbery and shooting, my husband John just about had apoplexy every time he thought about that bank. I'm sure all he could see in his imagination were robbers sneaking in the front door and murderers lurking in the closets. He referred to the place as a shooting gallery. He said there was no telling when the next robbery and murder were going to occur there."

She continued, "John felt his law practice was bringing in sufficient funds for us to get along well without my bank pay. He raved on and on claiming he couldn't sleep at night thinking of his Bobbie dodging bullets at the bank. Therefore, I sadly turned in my resignation and after two weeks left my delightful job. I will admit I've been quite happy having more time to volunteer for a couple of welfare organizations, and my tennis has improved at least fifty percent. It has improved so much that every once in a while I can return one ball in a row."

I then commented to Bobbie, "I surely understand and approve of John's attitude. Fiona works in her architecture office, a place of reasonable safely, but if she worked in a bank I would probably feel just as John did about your work at the First Universe Bank."

After I said this I must confess my thoughts turned to Fiona's activities in trying to solve crimes. In those cases she sometimes faced dangers I think far exceeded those in almost any bank you can name. I particularly remember a recent case where she shot a criminal, thus saving both our lives.

Chapter Seventeen

A Frightening Trip

On the next afternoon, a Sunday, Lt. Seabrook called to tell us of a new development in the case. On Sunday mornings the Manigaults would go to Sunday school and church at the Baptist Church on Jungle Road. (In Charleston they are members of the Huguenot Church.) After church they go to the Pavilion for lunch, as do a good many people who make their homes at Edisto or at least spend a few months there each year. As a result, they are away from their homes for several hours each Sunday morning.

When the Manigaults returned to their home they discovered it had been broken into and searched. In their backyard there are quite a few large bushes and trees that would have provided good cover for an intruder. (To me the front door of a beach house is the one facing the ocean.) The lock on the back door had been broken to gain entrance. The house seemed to have been searched carefully, but nothing of special value had been taken even though there was some cash and jewelry spread around. The thief had, however, taken a coast and geodetic survey map of the Edisto area from the wall in the front hall.

I understand Bobbie's room looked as though it had been torn apart whereas the rest of the house seemed to have been disturbed very little. When I asked Fiona how the thief would have known Bobbie's room from the others, she said it would have been very easy. The other occupied bedroom contained both male and female clothing, whereas Bobbie's room had just female clothing. We were also to learn that several letters addressed to Bobbie had been received since her disappearance. Sue Manigault had placed them, unopened, on Bobbie's dresser. These letters had been taken along with the area map. Nothing else seemed to have been taken from the house.

The police had spent a great deal of time checking the house for fingerprints. After much effort they concluded the intruder had been wearing gloves. We passed all this information on to Bobbie who agreed with Fiona and me that the person who broke in was trying to determine where Bobbie was hiding. She did not seem to be extremely worried, other than being concerned that Sue's house had been messed up, until we told her the map of the Edisto area had been stolen. She exclaimed, "Mainwaring Island is shown on that map and the murderer in all probability will see it and will head there to look for me!"

That afternoon Bobbie returned to her work on the five notebooks. After she had been diligently writing for about an hour she suddenly exclaimed, "Oh, my goodness! I have not thought to tell you about the notebook I was working on over at the island."

I questioned her, "What notebook is that?"

"Well, one of the things I had been doing to pass the time over there was to keep a diary of my activities in a loose leaf notebook. After you came over and said you would return to pick me up in two days, I continued the practice. I have suddenly realized that I included the two of you and Lt. Seabrook in my entries. If the murderer goes to the island, he may very well read my notes about the three of you."

Fiona asked, "In addition to our names did you write anything about our plans to disguise you and take you back to Edisto to stay with us? Also, where did you leave the book?"

Bobbie chokingly replied, "I'm afraid I did mention those things. I left the book on the kitchen table where I sat for much of my time on the island."

Fiona calmly said, "Well, Jack, that means you will have to borrow the Mainwaring boat and go to the island at high tide tomorrow to retrieve the notebook. Eventually in his efforts to locate Bobbie the killer will surely see or hear the name 'Mainwaring Island.' He will then easily be able to locate it on the map he took from the Manigaults. If that happens he will probably think there is a good possibility Bobbie is hiding there. From this, he will surely immediately go there to look for Bobbie. In that case I am sure he will either have another flounder gig or a gun with him along with a plan to eliminate Bobbie if he should find her.

"Furthermore," she continued, "he will not find Bobbie there but if he looks through the house he will surely find the notebook and carefully examine it. If that happens, I am sure he will return to Edisto looking for all three of us. Should he find us before we find him, the results will probably not be very pleasant. Jack, maybe you should go over tonight at high tide and not wait until tomorrow."

"Oh no!" I replied. "You don't have any idea of the difficulties involved in finding your way up the creek out in the marsh at night. It's almost impossible unless you've been in the area dozens of times and the difficulties are compounded when there is no moon which is the situation we have tonight. It will be almost pitch black dark, and all you would be able to see would be marsh grass on both sides of you and the stars above.

"Traveling along under those circumstances in the dark is almost like wandering along in a deep ditch with numerous intersecting ditches that all look alike. I've been lost in the marsh at night before and don't plan to let it happen again. I admit if I could find the place in the dark I could probably get out by going with the water flow after high tide, but I wouldn't try it. I will go over in the morning and see if I can find the diary. If I do, I will either bring it back here or destroy its contents, as you wish, Bobbie."

"Destroy them," she instructed.

From the tide tables I learned high tide would be at about 9:30 in the morning. You notice I said about 9:30 AM. The times of high and low tides at the ocean front can be obtained quite accurately from the tide tables but back in the marshes the times of high and low tides will be somewhat later and those delays can only be roughly estimated. Well, I got up at 7:30 AM, grabbed a banana and glass of orange juice, obtained the island house key from Bobbie, then headed to the marina. I took the boat and headed back to Mainwaring Island. It was so much easier to travel in daylight rather than on a moonless night. Once at the island I tied the boat to the old dock and walked to the house.

On our previous visits to the island we only stayed for short times so I did not go into the old ramshackle house. This time, however, I walked right in and, boy, was I in for a delightful surprise. The house had been turned into a wonderful hunting and fishing lodge. There were deer skins on the floors and even one bear rug. The walls were covered with antlers, stuffed fish, and fish and game pictures. The book cases were filled with hunting and fishing books while the cabinets were loaded with duck decoys. In the closets there were fishing rods, crab nets, and boxes of hooks, sinkers, corks, and fish lines. Oh, what a super place!

I now understood why every male (and that includes me) who ever walked into that house said it was the most wonderful and beautiful place he had ever seen. On the other hand, I understand that every woman who ever saw the place said it was the worst place she had ever seen.

I went into the kitchen where I found the notebook on the table as Bobbie had said. My next planned step was to burn the pages in an old wood stove in the kitchen, but just as I started to do so I heard the outboard motor of a nearby boat. As a result, I tore out the pages, stuffed them into my pocket, moved to the front of the house, and stood by a window to see if anyone was coming. Sure enough, in about ten minutes a man with a rifle came slowly walking up the trail. I tried to see if I could recognize him when suddenly I realized he was wearing a stocking mask over his face.

I decided retreat was the better part of valor and quickly slipped out the back of the house and ran into the jungle-like woods toward the back of the island. I then used my cell phone to call Fiona and tell her someone else was on the island so I was going to stay in hiding back in the woods until he left. I told her the next high tide would be after dark so I would plan to wait until the next morning to leave. In my rush I didn't give Fiona a chance to respond. At the end of my call I shut the phone off so there would be no incoming calls the sound of which might be heard by the other man on the island.

Suddenly, I heard the back screen door of the house slam. The intruder yelled, "Bobbie, I have a message for you from your husband. Where are you?"

At that moment I said a silent prayer of thanks that we had been allowed to find Bobbie and get her off the island a few days ago. I was sure this man had to be the killer for whom we had been looking.

I retreated a considerable distance further back into the island and hid in a thicket. After a little while I saw the man coming through the trees some distance away. He was headed in my general direction carrying his rifle at the ready. I knew if he found me, he would not hesitate to shoot me.

I moved slowly through the bushes and almost to the back of the island. There I debated in my mind between trying to climb a tree and hide there or to slip into another thicket. Finally, I decided to do neither. Instead I stepped down into one of the swamp ponds on the back of the island and waded over among some bushes in the edge of the water. I eased my way further and further out into the deeper water until it came up to just about my shoulders. I was very happy that I had my cell phone in its waterproof pouch! Fortunately, the bottom of the pond was fairly solid I guess due to the fact that it consisted mostly of sand. My fear had been that the bottom would consist of pluff mud as are most of the soils of salt marshes. If that had been the case, I would have found moving around to be almost impossible because I would sink a couple of feet down into the mud and find walking extremely difficult.

Anyway, I ducked down behind a bush with only my head above the water. To hopefully hide myself better I broke a rather large leafy limb from one of the bushes and held it in front of my face. I stayed in that pond for what seemed like two forevers. Well, at least for an hour or two. During that time I could hear the man going through the woods calling for Bobbie.

My greatest fear in the pond was the possible presence of an alligator or two. I have always heard (correctly, I hope) that alligators will not attack you unless humans have been feeding them. Apparently, they have a natural fear of humans, but if humans start feeding them they grow to expect it. This causes them to lose their fear, and they may very well attack. The reason I felt somewhat safe in the pond was I figured the Mainwarings were smart enough not to feed those creatures. Fortunately, I did not see a single alligator while I was in the pond, but I will admit every time I heard some noise in the water I almost had a heart attack. There were a few snakes in the pond, but they did not come near me.

Eventually, I heard the man go back into the woods and head toward the house. Nevertheless, I stayed where I was for some time for fear he was acting as though he was giving up the hunt but in reality was waiting in ambush to see if Bobbie would come out of hiding enabling him to shoot her. Anyway, for safety, I stayed in the pond for what seemed like several more hours but was probably only forty-five minutes or so.

As I stood there in the swamp in several feet of water, my thoughts returned to the original purpose of my trip out here, the retrieval or at least the destruction of Bobbie's island diary. I reached my hand in my pocket to remove the pages of the diary and found they were nothing but a soggy mess with the ink from the writing spread all over the pages so the words were unreadable. That was good news. Nevertheless, I struggled up out of the water and found a rock on the shore. I wrapped the soggy mess around the rock and pitched the result out into the pond. There it sank to its death in a watery grave. This action made me feel a little better because the purpose of my trip had now been achieved. I began to walk slowly along the shore of the pond. I think it's unnecessary to tell you that after all that time of standing motionless in the water my joints felt they were at the very least 90 years old and seemed as though they were so stiff they would never operate successfully again.

Realizing the masked stranger could not leave the island until the next high tide was almost in and that would be after dark, I did not walk anywhere near the house but stayed in the forest some distance away trying to stay hidden in heavily thicketed areas. After at least one eternity, I heard the start of an outboard motor and realized the man must be getting ready to leave. In the next few minutes the sound of the motor became steadily fainter until finally I could hear it no longer. Though it was dark, he could go with the outgoing tide. It was only then that I felt it was safe to cautiously walk toward the house. As the tide was quite high I could get in Bobbie's Yacht and leave the island. However, I was afraid to do this because I thought the killer might expect if anyone was on the island that would be exactly what he or she might do. Thus, he might be waiting somewhere downstream with his rifle ready to pick off anyone who came out.

My first order of business was to call Fiona to let her know I was still among the living. The waterproof pouch had done its job. My cell phone was still in working order even after being in the water so long, and I had no difficulty reaching her. When she answered I realized she had probably been anxiously sitting by the phone waiting for my call almost all day. I apologized for not calling sooner and said, "I had no alternative. If this man had heard me calling, I am sure I would have been shot."

I heard a groan on the other end of the phone.

Continuing I said, "I felt I could not call you until I was sure he had left the island. Though the tide is sufficiently high for me to get the boat out now, I am afraid to try it because the killer, and I'm sure that is who this man is, might be waiting downstream with his rifle in case anyone is on the island and tries to leave during the next hour or two while the tide is still high. Though I could get the boat out now, I am afraid to risk it.

"Would you please call Lt. Seabrook and ask if he or one of his men could come over and pick me up on the high tide tomorrow morning? If I were to take the Mainwaring boat back to the marina in the morning and should the killer be in that vicinity and see me and the boat, he would probably realize Bobbie was somewhere nearby and might very well follow me to the house. As a result, I think Bobbie's Yacht should be left over here for the present."

"OK, if you think that is the best plan," Fiona said with some hesitation. "I will call the lieutenant. But listen, Dodo, please be careful. Stay hidden and don't do anything stupid. I'm looking forward to hugging you tomorrow."

"Don't worry. I'll be fine," I told her while all I could think about was, "She even said 'Dodo' with tenderness. How nice!"

You will perhaps remember I only had a very light breakfast and no lunch on this day. As a result, I was almost hungry enough to try to catch an alligator and have him for supper hoping the reverse would not happen. Finally, I returned to the house where I found some cans of Campbell's soup and some rather limp saltine crackers. The directions on the can say it is necessary to add one can of water to each can of the concentrated soup. Though the water available on the island was that foul tasting sulphur water, I added it to the soup mix and heated it on the wood stove. I then devoured two cans of the stuff along with some of the soggy crackers.

Normally I am a person who loves a little solitude now and then, but being on this lonely island provided more solitude than I wanted. After some thought on the matter I decided to spend the night on Bobbie's Yacht where there were two bunks in the cabin. I found a flashlight in the kitchen to help me as I walked down to the boat.

After a long and lonely night, with a little sleep mixed in here or there, I got up at just about the same time as the sun. A few hours later I heard a motor boat coming up the stream. In some fear it might not be the police, I retreated into the nearby woods. Much to my delight I saw the boat manned by Lt. Seabrook and one of his officers coming around the curve in the creek. I returned to the dock and greeted them happily. I told them of my experiences the day before. At this time Lt. Seabrook sternly reminded me that we had promised to keep him informed of our activities in trying to solve this mystery.

He lectured, "You can see this foray nearly cost you your life. I fully expect you to live up to my rules in the future or there will be no more investigations for you in this case."

I apologized sincerely and said we had not kept him in the dark deliberately. We thought this would be such a simple task it had never occurred to us to notify him of what we were doing. Fortunately, he seemed satisfied by my explanation.

Anyway, they took me back to the marina where my car was parked. I drove to our house where I found two very worried looking girls waiting for me. Fiona gave me a warm welcoming hug and kiss. They fed me a glorious blueberry pancake breakfast, and Fiona actually shed a few tears when I described in detail my experiences on the island. Maybe there is a slight chance she may value me almost as much as she cares for her investigations of robberies, bloody murders, and those awful tennis racquets. I hope so.

As we sat around talking about my experiences the day and night before, Fiona suddenly exclaimed, "Hooray! We may now have the killer if he is an employee of the bank. All we have to do is check to see if anyone was absent from work at the bank yesterday. If so, and it was a man, he surely must be the killer."

Well, she called the bank and sadly found the murderer was still apparently one step ahead of us. All of the bank employees were away yesterday. We had been going through an unusually hot few days and the first arrivals at work that morning found the building was almost unbearably hot. The air conditioning and heating company that serviced the building was called and immediately sent some workmen over. They found someone had vandalized the outdoor condenser, fan and compressor. It would take them a whole day to repair them. As a result, the bank was closed and everyone was sent home. Well, we have been outsmarted again.

Chapter Eighteen

My Search for Bobbie Mainwaring

(As told by the second robber-murderer.)

My greatest desire for the last few years has been to retire and move to one of the Caribbean islands. I would like to purchase a little property on the seashore and construct a reinforced concrete home sufficient to resist the worst recorded hurricanes in that area. Then I would like to spend the rest of my life on that island swimming, sunbathing, snorkeling, golfing, fishing, and drinking rum and coke. It makes my mouth water just to think of such nonproductive activities.

The problem in carrying out these dreams has always been financial. Originally my plans for obtaining the necessary money were perfectly honest and ethical. I would make good solid investments in the stock market and quickly build up sufficient funds. I invested almost all of my cash in the shares of several major national banks thinking over a few years their values would double and redouble. Unfortunately, my shares fell like a rock during the recent recession and severely delayed the realization of my tropical dreams. I stupidly had no stops on my shares and just sat around watching them go through the floor thinking day by day their values would come bouncing back. This did not happen.

Although my present income is quite adequate to live on comfortably, my plans for a tropical future had seemingly been wiped out or at least delayed for many years. Soon after the nose dive of my stock market account I began to think of ways I could recoup my losses ethically or otherwise. One day I was reading a newspaper account of a bank robbery in Chicago. As I read, I began to think a good bank robbery would restore and increase my savings account and perhaps even provide me with all of the money necessary to begin living my dreams right away.

The only trouble with my new idea was that an armed robbery was out of the question for me. First of all, I lacked the courage to enter into such a venture. I'm sure if I did try it the police would catch me, and I would probably be shot or, worse, would have to serve a long prison sentence. However, as I continued to think about bank robberies I stumbled upon an idea for robbing the bank where I work. My idea, however, would only work if someone else committed an armed robbery of the bank first.

My idea began to develop. If my bank was robbed, I, as an insider, would be ready when the robbers departed from the bank to scoop up as much of the cash left in the bank as possible. If I could do this without being caught, no one need ever know there had been a second robbery if I played my cards right. The police would think all the money had been taken by the armed intruders. I would be in the clear and hopefully would be able to pick up enough cash to carry out my

Caribbean plans. But what would I do with the money when I grabbed it? Where would I put it, and how would I get it out of the bank? Those were the big problems.

One day as I sat dreaming of snorkeling in a clear tropical sea or playing tennis under the palm trees, a thought came to me for hiding the money in the bank itself rather than immediately taking it out and hiding it somewhere else. My plan, I thought, would enable me to hide the money so well that the police probably wouldn't be able to find it no matter how carefully they looked. Of course I didn't think they would ever search the bank in the first place because they would surely think all the missing money was taken by the armed robber. They would probably never know there had been a second robbery.

Well, one day our bank was robbed just as I had hoped would eventually happen. Unfortunately, one of our tellers was killed, something I had not hoped for. Anyway, I immediately put my much rehearsed plan into action and successfully took several hundred thousand dollars then hid it where I thought no one would find it. I took a large post office custom box (12″x12″x5 ½″), walked into the vault, and carefully looked to see if anyone was observing my activities. As no one seemed to be looking, I quickly grabbed stacks of the larger bills and tossed them into my box, filling it to the brim. Then I closed the box, walked back to my office, and shut the door. This whole process probably took about two minutes.

Back in my office I sat down at my desk and went to work rolling groups of 40 or 45 bills in tight rolls with diameters of one inch or less. On each roll I would put a piece of scotch tape to keep it from springing loose. I dropped each roll back into the box. When someone came into my office, I would close the lid of the box.

Should someone have discovered what I was doing (no one did) I would have said I was counting the money that remained in the vault. That would have ended my robbery plans as I would have had to return the money to the vault. At least in that case I wouldn't be charged with robbery.

The rolling of the bills took me at least two hours. Once that task was complete I proceeded to hade five rolls at a time in my secret hiding places that I had prepared several years in advance. I estimated that on average each set of five rolls contained ten to fifteen thousand dollars.

I thought I was completely in the clear, but then bad luck came along. That dratted armed robber had the gall to become deathly ill and on his death bed confess his robbery of the bank and the shooting of our teller. If he had said no more, I would still have been safe. But he, with his big mouth, had to tell how much money he had earned with his work at the bank on that day. Unfortunately for me, his confession revealed the fact that there had been a second robbery much larger than the first one. As a consequence, the police, apparently suspecting an inside job, searched the bank several times but found nothing.

I began to wonder if anything had happened that would point to me as the robber. I painstakingly tried to think of anything I had done before or after the robbery that would cast suspicion in my direction. There was only one thing I could ever think of that fell into this category. We used to employ a lovely secretary named Bobbie Mainwaring. One day before the robberies took place she came into my office and saw me behaving in what I would call a rather suspicious manner. At the time it probably would not have seemed suspicious to her, but if she thought back after the robberies to the incident and realized what I had been doing, my goose would have been cooked. (By the way, I sure would like to take that girl with me to my tropical island. There are, however, three large obstacles in the way of such a plan: her husband, my wife, and finally Bobbie wouldn't willingly go with me in the first place.)

Now that the whole world seemed to know there had been a second robbery at our bank, I began to think of the danger Bobbie posed to me. Perhaps if I could kill her, that would eliminate forever any chance of suspicion being directed at me. One day I was in our bank lobby when I heard two tellers who were friends of Bobbie talking about her. One of them said she had seen the dear girl a few days before. Bobbie had told her she was going to Edisto Beach for a couple of weeks to stay with her friends, the Manigaults. Fate surely seemed to be on my side at that time. I immediately began to plan to go to Edisto for the purpose of disposing of Bobbie.

My sister Elizabeth and her husband, Don, have a home on Jungle Shores Drive on the back of Edisto Beach. They now live in San Diego and seldom come to South Carolina any more. I have a key to their home, and they just tell me to use the place whenever I wish. In exchange they do expect me to keep an eye on the house and to do a little yard work now and then. As a result, I often go back and forth to Edisto and no records of my visits are kept as would be the case if I periodically rented a house there. My wife Estelle is so wrapped up in her social circle that she has almost no interest in ever going beyond the Charleston city limits except to visit a few fine and expensive nearby restaurants.

Upon arriving at the Edisto house, I looked up the Manigaults in the small local phone book and found their house was on Palmetto Boulevard by the ocean about one and one half miles south of the pavilion. Knowing Bobbie was a great early morning jogger, I got up the next day before the sun, put on a big floppy hat and sun glasses, drove to the pavilion, and walked a little to the north by the state park. It was my hope that this spot away from any houses would be along her jogging route.

Sure enough, Bobbie came jogging along the beach in a few minutes. She did not recognize me due to my glasses, hat and the fact that I turned my back to her as she jogged by. I resolved that she was only going to jog on this earth for one more day. Tomorrow I would return to this area and remove her and her danger to me. I returned to the house, dressed in my suit and tie, and drove to Charleston for my day's labor at the bank.

That evening I returned to Edisto. The next morning before sunup, I returned to the beach by the park. I put on my stocking mask and waited. Luck was with me as there was an extremely thick fog on the beach that morning. Soon I saw a young girl with black hair and about Bobbie's size jogging down the beach near me. I was prepared. She had to pass very close because the tide was fairly high thus only a narrow strip of the beach was out of the water. I again deliberately faced away from her, this time so she would not see I was wearing a stocking mask. I had my trusty three pronged gig with me and as soon as she passed I took a few quick running steps after her and plunged the gig in her back. I believe at the time I said something like, "I guess that will shut you up Bobbie Mainwaring." Fortunately, there was a very large sand castle nearby. I dragged her over to it and quickly pushed sand from the castle walls over her body.

Now, thinking my troubles were over, I returned to the house, changed my clothes, and headed back to the bank. It was the next day before I discovered I had killed the wrong girl. I stayed in Charleston for a few days and then started going back and forth to Edisto again. It was my plan to go to the beach early each morning to try to find and kill the real Bobbie. However, I soon learned from the newspapers and television that she had disappeared, and the police were looking for her just as I was. I lived in constant dread that she would remember that day at the bank when I was behaving in a somewhat suspicious manner.

In some way Bobbie must have realized she was the intended target of the gig. As a consequence, she vamoosed. During the days following her disappearance, the police, her husband, and various friends searched diligently for her on both the island and surrounding areas, but to no avail. After a few days of this activity I decided her Manigault friends would probably know where she was hiding. So one Sunday morning when I thought they would be going to church, I decided to break into their house to see if I could find any evidence as to her present whereabouts. I drove over to the vicinity of the Manigault house and parked in a public beach access point near their home. From that spot I could watch their house as I sat in my car. Sure enough they came out awhile later and drove off, I assumed to church. I immediately walked over to their house where I was able to break the lock on the backdoor with a crowbar. I allotted myself a maximum of one hour for searching the house. During this time the only thing I found interesting to me were some unopened letters addressed to Bobbie that I put in my pocket. Later when I opened and read them they provided no clues as to her present location. Finally, on the way out I saw an interesting topographic map of the Edisto area on the wall. I took it with me as I left the house.

After returning to the house of my sister and her husband, I idly began to look over the topographic map paying little attention until suddenly I saw an island to the southwest of the beach out in the marshes named "Mainwaring." Could that land belong to the Mainwaring family? Could that be where Bobbie was hiding?

The next day I was supposed to be working at the bank, but I wanted to take the day off to go to Mainwaring Island and see if Bobbie was there. If she was, it would be an easy matter to dispose of her. If, however, I skipped work that day and Bobbie was killed, it might direct suspicion in my direction if all the bank employees were on duty except me. This would be particularly true if it could be shown I had been spending the night at Edisto.

As I thought about this problem I decided if I were to go to the bank and disable the air conditioning system nobody would be able to work in the place the next day because of the heat wave we had been enduring lately. Thus my absence would not be noticed. Accordingly, I drove to Charleston late that night, parked my car at a shopping center two blocks from the bank, and walked the rest of the way. I carefully sneaked up to the condenser unit with its fan and compressor, snipped all the wires and quietly removed some parts of the equipment. I had to be very careful not to be seen by the night watchman who was probably sound asleep in the building. I then returned to Edisto.

A salt creek comes up behind my sister's house. By the creek there is a boathouse with a runabout that can easily be pushed into the creek at all but the lowest tides. Well, the next morning I pushed the boat out of the boathouse and took off for the island. I had waited until the tide was nearly in before I left because I realized there might be trouble getting through the marsh at lower tides. Upon arriving at the island, I saw a cabin boat by the dock with the name "Bobbie's Yacht" painted on the side. Surely, I thought, I must have come to the right place. I grabbed my rifle and climbed aboard the yacht but found no one was in the cabin. Nevertheless, I felt Bobbie must be somewhere nearby on the island.

I climbed onto the dock and walked up a path through the forest. Finally I came to an old house. Since the front door was unlocked, I went in and searched each of the rooms. Though I found no one, I surely thought somebody must be here on the island. The house looked as though someone had been living there. I next started looking around the forest but had no luck there either. By the time I finished this search, the tide was dead low. Unfortunately that meant I had to wait several hours before I could get out of that creek. I decided to sit with my rifle in some bushes behind the house to see if anyone came along. I sat there for several hours with no luck. Finally, just after dark the tide was pretty high again. I decided to leave the island. It is extremely difficult to find your way through the marshes in the dark, but in this case I was able to go with the flow of the tide. I finally got down to the entrance of Jefford Creek. I stopped a little way around a curve in the much larger Fish Creek with my rifle at the ready and sat there for a while thinking if Bobbie had been hiding on the island she might try to leave the island on this high tide. If she did so, I planned to pick her off with my rifle when she came by and then return to Edisto and Charleston.

Unfortunately, no one came along. After an hour or two, I gave up and left. I'll have to try this again during the weekend. On that trip I'll go in before the tide is completely high but cut off the motor before I get to the island. Then I can paddle quietly and float in with the rising tide. I will slip onto the island and hide in the forest near the house and wait for hours if necessary to see if Bobbie is there. If she is, I'll shoot her and proceed back to Charleston to continue the work on my Caribbean house plans now that I have sufficient funds for the project.

Chapter Nineteen

A Treasure Hunt

One afternoon the three of us were playing half ball on the beach. This is a game, fairly common on South Carolina beaches, where you play baseball with a sponge rubber ball that is cut in half. The half ball is pitched to a batter who uses a broom handle as the bat. The ball is quite difficult to hit because the pitcher can get a curve of several feet or pitch a ball that wobbles all over the place. I think the best way to hit the speedily curving and/or wobbling ball is to hold the broom handle in one hand when you swing.

While the three of us were playing, a young man about Bobbie's age named Billy Guillebeau (pronounced GILL-LIE-bow) came up and asked if he could join us in the game. We were happy to have him because he seemed to be a very pleasant geechie, and we needed another fielder. I, however, noticed Bobbie seemed to be keeping her distance from this young fellow and almost seemed to be shielding her face from his view. After he had been playing with us for a little while, he walked over to Bobbie and said, "Hello, Bobbie. When did you start bleaching your hair?"

All this time we thought we had her disguised so well her own mother would not recognize her. Now the first old acquaintance of hers who comes along recognizes her immediately.

Bobbie replied, "Billy, please forgive me for being so standoffish. I thought I was so well disguised that no one I knew would recognize me with my blonde hair and big sun glasses. Yet you seemed to know me at first glance. How did you do it?"

Billy smiled, "As soon as I saw you I recognized your pretty face. Before I spoke to you a moment ago, however, I wanted to make sure it was you by looking to see if you had a scar on the back of your left leg from climbing over that barbed wire fence so many years ago. And sure enough, there it was. I never had the feeling you were being uppity because of some society level you may have obtained. I realized good old Bobbie had a reason for the way she was behaving."

"Billy, it's good to see you as always but please don't tell anyone you have seen me. Otherwise I might get murdered as a result. Last year I was working as a secretary at First Universe Bank there in town when it was robbed those two times. We think the man who carried out the second robbery there is trying to kill me because he thinks I can identify him. He has already made one attempt even though the truth is I have no idea who he is or what he looks like. This explains why I am disguised, although apparently not very well."

Billy stepped over and hugged Bobbie. He promised he would tell no one about seeing her, but he did tell Bobbie she should do a better job with her disguise, particularly the scar on her leg. (Fiona and I were both distressed over his remarks concerning her do-over work on Bobbie's appearance.) For one thing we had not given a thought to the prominent scar on her leg.

We played half ball for a little while longer, took a short dip in the ocean and headed back to our house, but only after we made sure Billy Guillebeau was not in sight. We didn't want anyone to know where Bobbie was staying.

After we had showered and had supper we huddled in the living room trying to decide how to change Bobbie's looks even further than we had and even whether we should move her to some other place to hide. After much discussion we decided to revise her disguise somewhat, to trust Billy not to tell anyone he had seen Bobbie, and to stay in the same house we had been renting. Bobbie agreed to dye her hair brown and to wear it up on top of her head. I guess you call that a "top knot." She and Fiona found in an island store a stain for instant sun tan. It's true that Bobbie already had an excellent sun tan, but the white scar on her leg stood out very clearly. However, a couple of applications of this artificial stain covered it up quite well. Despite these changes, her face was still a problem. Finally, we were able to change its looks by putting a rather small bandage tightly taped on her right cheek. This seemed to distort her face so it looked quite different, at least to us.

We completed the new disguise work and moved out to the rocking chairs on the front porch. I confess I was still not too sure Bobbie was disguised sufficiently to enable her to avoid being recognized if she should encounter another old acquaintance or worse if she were seen by the man we were trying to locate who had robbed the bank and killed the girl on the beach.

While sitting there on the porch, we started talking about what we were going to do the next day. I suggested we spend the day looking for old Spanish silver and gold on the island. I said we knew the pirates operated up and down the Carolina coast and at one time even blockaded the port of Charleston. Before we left home and made our trip down to Edisto, I had faked an old pirate treasure map. As a result I claimed the pirates must have buried much treasure on the offshore islands of the Carolinas. I showed the girls the map and claimed I had found it in a 200-year old book I had bought in a bookstore back home.

In several places on the Internet I had read how to prepare a fake treasure map and make it seem old and authentic. According to these excellent sources, the first step in faking an old map was to draw the map on a sheet of white paper and then to roughly tear off all the edges of the paper.

The next step involved wiping both sides of the map with a wet tea bag to cause the paper to turn brown and thus old looking. Then the paper was crumpled and allowed to dry for a day or two. As a third and final step, cooking oil was wiped on both sides of the map and the map was dried with paper towels.

You will note on my map and in the directions the term "rood" (also called a rod or perch) is used. This is a term used at one time by the English as a unit of distance. It was equal to 16.5 feet, supposedly the length of the pole or rod used for driving oxen. So when the directions say ten roods that means 10 x 16.5=165 feet.

Well, I showed the resulting map to two very skeptical girls, Fiona and Bobbie. Despite their suspicions of the authenticity of my beautiful map, they agreed to accompany me on this expedition the next morning. I had brought to the beach two shovels, a 100 foot steel tape, and several wood stakes to be used in the hunt. The directions on true pirate maps of 250 or 300 years ago were usually written in Olde English, but I had written them in present day English. I'm sure this fact increased the feelings of these two girls that I was a faker. I showed Fiona and Bobbie the directions and map for finding the treasure.

Pirate flag

On this the fifteenth day of September in the year of our Lord 1717, we were proceeding north toward Ocracoke on the good ship Queen Anne's Revenge. I buried on this day 2000 gold escudos and 1000 silver pieces of eight in a chest on Oristo Island off the southern Carolina coast.

To locate the treasure you begin on the south side of Scott Creek on Oristo Island where the high water marks for the creek and the front beach coincide. At that point you proceed 10 roods inland along the creek high water mark and there you place a wooden peg. Then you return to your starting point. From there you proceed 20 roods to the south along the ocean high water mark.

From that point you move 10 roods inland on a line perpendicular to the shore and place another peg. The treasure is buried midway between the two set pegs. After the chest was buried, I, of necessity, disposed of my two helpers and returned alone to the ship.

Signed and sealed by
Edward Teach

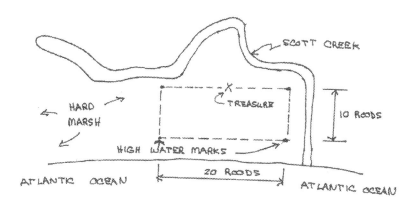

Location of Hidden Treasure

At the top of the map and directions a Jolly Roger flag is shown. This was a type of flag frequently used to identify pirate ships. There are several explanations of the origin of the term "Jolly Roger." Perhaps the most common explanation is that the term comes from the French words "jolie rouge" that actually mean "pretty red." These words referred to a plain red flag used on some pirate ships to indicate the crew would fight to the last man in any conflict. One of the other theories for the origin of Jolly Roger is that it came from the devil's nickname "Old Roger."

I have always hoped some day to find on one of my trips to Edisto an old Spanish doubloon lying in the sand waiting for me. It seems that should eventually happen since pirates so frequently sailed up and down this coast and since a number of their ships were sunk nearby. Unfortunately, there are many other persons with exactly the same thoughts who might get to my doubloon before I do.

During the days when pirates were so common in the Atlantic and the Caribbean, Spain commonly minted coins in both silver and gold. The silver ones were called "reales," and the gold ones were called "escudos." Both the reale and the escudos weighed roughly one eighth of an ounce each. An eight reale silver coin was called a "piece of eight" and had the number eight stamped on it. It weighed about one ounce and was sometimes called a "peso."

The correct meaning of the word "doubloon" is quite confusing. In Spanish the word means to double; thus, a doubloon is a coin of double value. But that definition doesn't really tell us what a doubloon is. As you move from the smallest Spanish coins of that day to the larger and larger coins, each one doubles the value of the last one. Therefore, by this definition any of the coins other than the smallest ones could be called doubloons.

The possession of gold coins was rare among the common people of Spain. The doubloon as we can now see didn't have any official value and the average person often just called any gold coin a doubloon. Our encyclopedias disagree on their definition of a doubloon. One of them says it's an eight escudo gold coin weighing about one ounce, while another says it's a two escudo gold coin weighing about one fourth of an ounce.

The Spanish coins of that day were handmade and hammered out to the thicknesses desired. They were not perfectly round. After they were cut to the approximate desired sizes, their weights were checked. If they weighed too much, some of the metal was nipped off making the coins even more irregular in shape. In this sketch you can see some of the shapes of a few old Spanish coins as they were recovered from sunken Spanish ships. From these shapes you can see that in a search for old Spanish coins you should not limit your thoughts only to perfectly round coins.

Shapes of some old Spanish coins

Well, we took the shovels and the map and began the approximately two mile walk from our house up the beach to the north and past the state park on to Scott's Creek. As we walked I kept talking about the location of the treasure buried in the sand so long ago. I told Fiona and Bobbie how the location of the creek, the shore, and the high water marks of the ocean and the creek were constantly changing through the years due to the action of the tides as well as the storms. I said we really had no idea where the creek and ocean had been nearly three centuries before. I would guess much of the land had washed away during that time, and the treasure was in all probability much nearer to the water (if not in it) than it had been when it was buried.

Nevertheless, we carefully followed the directions I had prepared. But despite much digging we found no reales or escudos. However, we did find two items that were quite surprising to me. The first thing was an old rusty flounder gig that gave me the cold shivers as I thought of what had happened to Martha Ulmer on the beach that day. I told the girls that Edward Teach (Blackbeard) had used this particular gig to dispose of his two helpers after they finished burying the treasure.

Fiona said to me, "Your imagination does run away with you sometimes."

I replied, "Is it my imagination that I am here on this lovely day with the two prettiest girls within four million roods? That's 12,500 miles by the way and includes just about every spot on this planet."

Fiona replied, "I'm sure you are right but, modestly speaking, it's only 3.5 million roods."

The second thing we found was the skeleton of a human hand. We placed it in a plastic bag and took it to Lt. Seabrook. He didn't seem particularly interested as he said such items were found on the island every once in a while.

After dismissing our find, he told us he had been trying to reach us all morning. He said Captain La Roche had called to say he had again investigated the five male employees of the bank and could find no suspicious behavior by any of them on the day and night I was on Mainwaring Island.

As we left the police station we saw some workmen out front drilling into and breaking up the pavement as they always seem to be doing in almost any town or city you can name. As we watched them, I noticed Bobbie seemed to be absolutely fascinated by their activities. She stood dreamily staring at the holes the men were drilling.

I asked, "Bobbie, what do you find so interesting about this work?"

She replied that she didn't know what it was, but the drilling reminded her of something in the back of her mind. She just didn't know what it was.

Chapter Twenty

Holes and More Holes

As we couldn't think of a particular line of investigation, the next day after breakfast the three of us decided to walk down the beach to the south for a couple of miles. Every few hundred yards in our walk we would have to hike up to the top of the beach to get around a groin. After we had done this several times, Bobbie said, "I have been to Edisto many times in my life, but I've never really understood how these groins work. I realize in some way they are supposed to keep the beaches from washing away, aren't they?"

Fiona groaned knowing a lecture was coming. But I cleared my throat and in my best professorial manner gave a lecture on the subject of beach erosion. "Bobbie, you are absolutely right as to the purpose for the groins. The U.S. Army Corps of Engineers have estimated that at least ninety percent of our beaches on the Atlantic coast are being severely eroded. Furthermore, the level of the ocean is very gradually rising due to the melting of the polar ice caps plus the sediment that is carried by our streams and rivers and deposited into the ocean. These actions mean our coastal land is gradually being submerged. I understand the rise is running about 4.5 inches per century. This means a large part of Edisto only has a few more centuries left before it will be under water.

"One of the several methods used to attempt to reduce beach erosion has been the construction of these walls, called groins, perpendicular to the shore line running from up on the beach on out into the edge of the ocean. They are used in an attempt to control or at least reduce erosion by slowing the sidewise movement of the water close to the shore." I drew a sketch in the sand to show her what I meant.

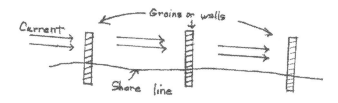

Groins used to help preserve and build up beach

"The major ocean current close to the shores of the beaches in South Carolina and adjoining states is from north to south. The Gulf Stream is further out in the ocean and is flowing in a northeasterly direction toward the British Isles. In efforts to protect beaches from erosion many communities have built groins such as the ones at Edisto. The groins are actually walls built with treated timber or concrete or even rock. The north-south current comes along transporting a good amount of sand. The water near the shore hits the groins and is slowed down. As it slows down, much of the sand it is transporting sinks to the bottom. Thus the buildup is usually on the north sides of the groins. You can walk along the beach here and see the sand is normally appreciably higher on the north sides of the groins than on the south sides. At least that's true for almost all of the groins. For a few of them, however, the direction of the shoreline and the swirling of the current due to various factors may cause the sand to be deposited so that it is deeper on the south sides of the groins.

"One disadvantage of groins is their interception of the sand carried by the water may very well cause a deprivation of the sand going toward the land further down the shore. Several other methods are used to try to prevent beach erosion and/ or to build up beaches. Included are breakwaters out from the shore, pumping sand from the ocean bottom well out from the shore onto the beach (probably the most successful and popular method used today), snow fences up on the shore to catch blowing sand, and planting sea oats to catch and hold sand much as do snow fences."

Fiona took a deep breath, "Is the lecture over, Professor?"

"Yes, for now," I answered. "But be prepared. You never know when the time will be right for a good lesson."

Fiona groaned again.

As you walk along the beach you will often see approximately two inch diameter holes dug by the ghost crabs. Their name comes from their very pale (almost ghostly) or sand color and from the fact that they generally only come out of their holes at night or at dusk. They are also called sand crabs. Bobbie seemed to be mesmerized by these holes just as she had been the day before by the drilling of the holes in the pavement over near the police station. As she stared at the holes, Fiona asked, "Bobbie, why are you so fascinated by these ghost crab holes in the beach? I am sure you have seen tens of thousands of them during your life. Have you always been fascinated by them?"

Bobbie replied, "You know, I have seen them all my life but only today I seem to be particularly interested in them. I don't understand it but they remind me of something in my past. Something about holes. It is like this thing deep in my brain that I know I need to remember but I can't bring to the surface. It is very similar to the times I have tried to remember someone's name from the past. It bugs me over and over but suddenly the name hits me. I hope whatever is buried is my brain concerning holes will hit me soon."

Fiona tried to help. "Suppose I name different types of holes that I can think of. Tell me if any of them bring back anything to you. There are bullet holes, key holes, donut holes, golf green holes or cups, swimming holes, bolt holes, pot holes, black holes, sink holes, post holes, button holes, watering holes, drill holes, fishing holes, and so on. Do any of these bring back anything to you?"

Bobbie thought about each of these holes and said with frustration, "No. Probably this whole idea about holes amounts to nothing, but it's driving me crazy trying to figure out why all of a sudden I am fascinated by holes."

Chapter Twenty-One

Some of the Stolen Money Surfaces

One day we were wandering along the beach looking for fossils and soaking up the sun when Fiona's cell phone rang. The call was from Captain La Roche asking if we would mind stopping by his office again when we had a chance. He said he had just obtained some information that might appreciably affect our investigations. Fiona told him we would drive into Charleston that afternoon to see him. After lunch we left Bobbie in the house telling her to keep trying to think about holes. Then we drove back to the city.

When we were seated in Captain La Roche's office he told us that two days before the robberies the preceding year, the bank had received a shipment of new one hundred dollar bills. As a result, they had a list of the numbers of those bills. A good many of them were taken during the robberies. After the robberies the First Universe Bank had provided the police and other banks with the numbers of those stolen bills. Captain La Roche said on the day before a bank over on Broad Street reported to the police that they had received six of the known stolen hundred dollar bills. Upon receiving this news, the captain immediately went over to the bank to learn how they got the bills. They told him a very respected owner of an antique store on King Street had made a deposit that contained six of the stolen bills. Captain La Roche said he immediately went over to the store in question to ask the owner where he got the bills.

The owner, Mr. Lafitte, said a lady from Indiana had come in that morning and bought an old English tea caddy and a pair of red and white Staffordshire dogs. She had paid him with eight one hundred dollar bills. He said he had given her a receipt and asked her where she was staying. She replied that she and her husband were at the round Holiday Inn over on the other side of the Ashley River on U.S. Highway 17.

Captain La Roche continued, "We drove over there and located her with no difficulty. At first she seemed very much afraid we were going to charge her with passing counterfeit bills. I assured her the bills she had spent were perfectly good, though stolen, and all we wanted to know was where she had obtained them. She explained how she had cashed a check for $1000 over at the First Universe Bank on Meeting Street, and they gave her ten $100 bills. I asked her to show me the other two bills. I checked them against the serial number list of stolen bills, but they were not on it. I thanked her for cooperating with us in our investigation and apologized for frightening her. I explained the bills had been stolen from a bank, and we were just trying to follow them back to the robber.

"We next went over to the First Universe Bank to determine the name of the teller who had cashed the $1000 check. A female teller, Lottie Rutledge, said she had cashed the lady's bank check with what appeared to her to be well circulated bills. She said she understood the stolen bills were crisp, new bills so it had never occurred to her to check the numbers on these wrinkled, rather dirty bills.

"Anyway, a search was made of all the $100 bills the bank had on hand, but no other stolen ones were found. No one in the bank could or would tell where those six bills had been obtained."

Fiona commented, "Well, we are back to square one. We still don't know whether the stolen money was left in the bank after the robbery or taken out."

Here I asked, "If these bills were left hidden in the bank, how could they have become mixed up with the bank's cash?"

Fiona answered, "Suppose you worked for the bank and had a stack of new one hundred dollar bills you had stolen from the bank. You knew the authorities had serial numbers for all of those bills, thus preventing you from spending them. You would surely hate the fact that you couldn't spend those beautiful bills. So what would you do? I tell you what I would do if I worked in the bank. I would first rough up and rub the bills in the dirt and then put some of them in my pocket. As I worked and moved around the bank, if I saw some good well used $100 bills, I would sneak a few of the tainted bills out of my pocket and swap them for the safe ones. If these bills were passed out to a customer and traced back to the bank, the bank could honestly say they had no idea how they got them."

Captain La Roche remarked, "I think you have a very reasonable hypothesis as to what happened. I, for one, am pleased these bills showed up. After listening to your idea about slipping the bills into the bank's other one hundred dollar bills, I am now sure the robber works for the bank. Furthermore, we already know he is male because Bobbie

Mainwaring saw him kill Martha Ulmer over at Edisto Beach. Then you were pursued over on Mainwaring Island by a man who in all probability works in the bank."

As we sat there looking at each other, I'm sure we were all thinking the same thing, "What do we do next?"

Chapter Twenty-Two

A Clue Remembered

O nly a few more days were left in our long vacation at Edisto Beach. The beach part of the trip had been super, but our investigations of the sand castle murder and the second bank robbery had been almost complete flops. Our one accomplishment had been finding and protecting Bobbie Mainwaring, but the danger to her was still present. We still did not know where or from whom it was coming. Neither did we know why it was coming.

We were sitting in the rocking chairs on our front porch one afternoon looking out over the ocean watching the pelicans dive. They would be flying low over the water when suddenly they would dive into the ocean and grab a poor innocent fish. There must have been a large school of fish near the shore on this day because there were so many pelicans flying back and forth. As we watched, I started complaining about the fact that our vacation was about to end and moaning I would never own that wonderful old swan neck golf club that was in residence at the bank in Charleston.

Fiona chimed in to make fun of my sad comments by moaning in a very exaggerated manner that she would never be able to hang those exquisite (ridiculous) old tennis racquets, also residing at the same bank, on the walls of our den back home.

Fiona then, as she had done on previous occasions, questioned Bobbie in detail about her work at the bank.

"How long," she asked, "has Mr. Rivers had those beautiful old tennis racquets and that ugly old golf club in his office? Do you know where he got them?"

Bobbie replied, "One day about two years ago he brought the racquets into the bank and had those glass cases installed to display them. My thought when I first saw them was that his wife didn't want them sitting around in her spic and span house. I assumed they didn't fit in with the décor she desired or something. About six months later Mr. Rivers brought that junky old golf club into the bank and hung it on the wall in his office. At the time I had the impression he had just purchased it at an antique store."

She hesitated for a moment and then suddenly added, "Now I remember the elusive something that's been running around in the back of my brain! But now that I remember what it was, it seems almost too insignificant to even mention."

When Fiona and I both excitedly asked her to tell us what it was she said, "Do you remember the other day when I was staring at the workmen drilling holes in the pavement as though I was in a trance? Then I looked at the crab holes on the beach. I couldn't figure out what information was buried in my brain. Well, looking at those holes and now hearing Fiona's question about the old tennis racquets and the golf club in Mr. Rivers' office must be what brought back my memory. One day when I entered Mr. River's office he had taken off the ends of the handles of two or three of the tennis racquets. I didn't even think the ends came off of those old racquets. I thought the handles were solid pieces of wood and yet the ones on his desk were hollow. Each of them had a fairly large circular hole, perhaps one inch or more in diameter, going up into the handle from its end. For some reason Mr. Rivers seemed to be embarrassed over the fact that I had seen him working on those racquets during office hours, and he hastily placed them on the floor under his desk. It was hard for me to understand why he was so upset on that particular day. I had seen him playing around with his tennis racquets on quite a few occasions in the past, and he hadn't seemed to be concerned in the least that I had observed his non-banking activities."

Hollow handled wooden tennis racquet (so what?)

At that moment I heard a sudden intake of breath and looked over at Fiona. I had never seen her so intent as she stared open mouthed at Bobbie. She moaned, "Why didn't I think of that long ago?"

Suddenly she turned back to face the ocean and began rocking furiously. I looked over at Bobbie and put one finger on my lips to request her silence.

For about half an hour there was dead silence other than the ocean's roar and the sound of Fiona's rocker rapidly going back and forth. She suddenly jumped out of her chair and excitedly shouted, "Bobbie, you have enabled us to solve the mysteries concerning the robbery and the murder! I love you!"

She rushed over and hugged a bewildered Bobbie then apparently as an afterthought said, "I love you too, Dodo," and she hugged me.

Bobbie and I were quite baffled by the situation and Bobbie asked, "What did I do? I don't have a clue about the name of the robber-murderer."

Fiona excitedly continued "I'm going to put my wonderful tennis racquets on our den wall near the large bookcase."

I injected a thought, "Suppose they don't suit my décor there?"

Ignoring my wise question, Fiona continued, "They will look great. You can put that awful old wooden New Zealand golf club under the house with the rest of your useless junk."

Bobbie and I both thought Fiona was taking our defeats in trying to solve these mysteries so hard that she had temporarily gone off her rocker. I told her in no uncertain terms that those cruddy racquets and the superb golf club belonged to Mr. Rivers. We couldn't just go pick them up as though they were ours and depart with them or else we both might end up behind prison bars.

In response to my sensible remarks Fiona said, "Yes, we can! Let's go to the Holy City tomorrow after breakfast and pick up those gorgeous racquets and, if you insist, that ugly golf club."

Then she said to Bobbie, "What did Mr. Rivers spend his time doing immediately after the armed robbery and murder?"

After thinking for a while, Bobbie responded, "He asked the tellers to very carefully count the money they each had in their booths while he counted the money in the bank vault. He spent some time there although he would frequently go over to his office. I assumed those trips were made to answer the phone or to make outgoing calls or perhaps to make notes as to the amount of money in the vault. Maybe those were calls to and from the insurance company as well as from members of the bank's Board of Directors. I could not actually hear or see what he did in his office because on that day he would close his door each time he went in."

Fiona then said to me quite clearly, "That broken down wood shaft golf club you love so much and those beautiful tennis racquets will be ours tomorrow thanks to Bobbie. By her words she has enabled us to solve this case! Now we can pick up those antiques and carry them home with us. Bobbie will be able to return to her husband sometime tomorrow."

At these words Bobbie jumped out of her chair like a jack in the box and almost shouted, "Fiona, may I dye my hair black tonight and borrow one of your fancy dresses and a pair of nice shoes to wear home to John? I don't want him to be ashamed of me with this brown hair and these beat up clothes and shoes."

Fiona told her of course she could do those things but not until we came back from Charleston the next afternoon. She told Bobbie not to worry because she was so pretty her husband would be proud of her if she showed up wearing a croker sack. (In South Carolina and neighboring states a croker sack is a term frequently used to describe a sack made from some coarse material such as burlap. These sacks are sometimes called crocus sacks or gunny sacks or burlap sacks in other parts of the country.)

Fiona next called Lt. Seabrook asking him if he could go with us to the First Universe Bank in the morning. She said we could definitely identify the person who had murdered the girl on the beach and had committed the second robbery at the bank. In addition she stated we would provide proof of our claims.

Lt. Seabrook indicated he would make time for such a trip and would bring along his pistol and a pair of handcuffs. Fiona told him it would be necessary to have Captain La Roche and one or two of his men on hand there to assist in the arrest. She further said he and the captain could work out their jurisdictional problems between themselves concerning who would make the actual arrest. She also told him this time we might run into some resistance to our searching the bank, and she thought it would be absolutely necessary to have a search warrant in case that happened.

"Please pass that on to the captain. I do not think we should make this trip until he has the warrant in his possession."

After Fiona hung up the phone, Bobbie asked if she could go with us. However, Fiona replied, "I'm afraid not. Your presence might possibly tip off the guilty party, and he might be able to escape. If everything goes well, Jack and I will call John and tell him to pick you up tomorrow evening. That is, if you are willing to part with our company and exchange it for his."

Bobbie sat there thinking for a while. I guess she was trying to think of a way to politely tell us we could go jump in the ocean if we thought she was going to stay with us instead of going home to her husband. Finally she said she hoped our feelings would not be hurt if she chose John's company over ours. She said she felt it was her duty to return to her husband.

In the morning Lt. Seabrook picked us up in his patrol car at the appointed time, and we headed to the Holy City. Along the way Fiona, much to my surprise, asked that she be allowed to run into a drug store for a moment. We found one on the outskirts of the city and stopped. Fiona rushed into the store and quickly returned with several pairs of tweezers. As she didn't seem to want to tell us the reason for her purchase, we continued our journey to the bank arriving there at about 10:00 AM. Captain LaRoche and several of his men were waiting for us.

Fiona addressed the group of policemen outside the bank saying we had solved the case and wanted them to be there to make the arrest. Both Lt. Seabrook and Captain La Roche agreed if we solved the case, it would take quite a load from their shoulders.

Fiona continued, "Jack and I want you people to claim credit for solving the case. Please keep our names out of it. There is, however, one thing we would like from you."

After being asked what that was, she explained, "If you have any other difficult cases and would like us to give them a try, please give us a ring."

Both officers agreed wholeheartedly to do so if we correctly solved the present case.

Fiona continued, "Our trouble in solving the case was, until recently, we thought the money had to have been taken out of the bank at the time of the robbery or shortly afterward. We could never figure how it could have been done no matter how hard we tried. This morning I would like to show you how I'm convinced the money has never left the bank. We will show you where the money is hidden and identify the person who is both the second robber and the murderer of the girl on the beach at Edisto.

"Now let's go into the bank and see Mr. Rivers. Please tell him we would like to search the bank one more time starting with his office. Please ask him to go out into the bank and leave us alone to conduct our search. He probably is tired of seeing us and might ask if we have a search warrant. Have two of your men go with him to keep him from leaving the bank."

At this point Captain La Roche asked, "What if he insists on leaving?"

Fiona responded, "If he does, arrest him for robbery and murder."

Well, we trooped into the president's office and explained our mission of searching the bank again. Mr. Rivers was not too happy. "We are trying to operate a bank and not have the police and these amateur detectives running in and out all the time. This time I demand that you show me your search warrant."

After this was done, he grudgingly said, "All right, but you aren't going to find anything."

Fiona asked him, "If we do find the money and solve the case, do we still get that cruddy old golf club and my pick of four of the old tennis racquets in the glass cases?"

In a rather sour manner Mr. Rivers replied, "In that case, you can have them all."

I think Fiona wanted to have witnesses to his promise about those antique items. I do not think, however, she expected him ever, even in a month of Sundays, to say, "Take them all." I could see she was elated. (Oh me, I thought, there are so many of these racquets there may not be enough room left in our house even in the basement for my splendid old golf clubs.)

As soon as Mr. Rivers left the office, Fiona handed a pair of tweezers to each of us. She then rushed over to the glass case and grabbed an armful of racquets. She passed two or three of them to each of us and asked us to pull and/or twist off their ends.

We did as she requested. The caps on the end of each racquet came off without too much trouble. Then she asked us to look into the holes and if they had something in them to take the tweezers and try to pull some of it out. Much to our surprise the floor was soon covered with $20, $50, and $100 bills. (Actually there were additional rolls of bills further up in the handle holes, but we couldn't reach those with the tweezers. They would have to be removed later.

"Hooray!" the police officers shouted in glee. "You have found the money!"

In some alarm I rushed over behind the president's desk and grabbed the New Zealand swan neck golf club to see if the end would come off. Fortunately, it did not. I then tapped the handle end on the floor to see if it sounded hollow, but it seemed to be solid. My fear was that he might have drilled a hole in it to hide some of the money. If that had been done, it would have probably taken away a great deal of the value of the club.

Captain La Roche and Lt. Seabrook had a little conference about jurisdiction and finally decided the captain would arrest Mr. Rivers and have him taken to the Charleston jail. I had been wondering whether the captain or the lieutenant would make the arrest—the Edisto police with a murder charge or the Charleston police with a charge of robbery. I guess they agreed they had the complete goods on the bank president for the robbery but had not yet clearly shown he was the murderer of the girl on the beach at Edisto.

Captain La Roche went out of the office and told his men to quietly arrest Mr. Rivers and take him to police headquarters on a charge of bank robbery. When he returned to the office, he and Lt. Seabrook heaped praise on Fiona and me for solving the case.

"Thank you for your kind words, but I feel I have done next to nothing. Fiona and Bobbie should get all the credit for finding the answers to the mysteries."

The arrest was made so quietly I don't think any of the bank employees realized anything had happened. As a result, Captain La Roche asked George Mengedoht, the vice president, to go into Mr. Rivers' office with him. There he explained the situation. Mr. Mengedoht seemed to be completely astounded and could not believe his friend James Rivers could have done these things. In any case the captain asked Mr. Mengedoht to take over the bank. Captain La Roche also asked him to contact the senior bank officials and the insurance company to explain the situation to them.

We asked the police officers if we could take our golf club and tennis racquets back to Edisto. They explained they would have to keep them for some time as evidence in the upcoming court case but would send them to us as soon as possible after the trial was over.

Before leaving the bank I called John Mainwaring's office. When his receptionist answered the phone, I asked her, "Are you the beautiful girl who allowed me to speak to Mr. Mainwaring a few days ago without an appointment?"

She replied that she was the girl who allowed me to speak to him, but she wasn't sure about the beautiful part. She then asked, "Are you that old fogey college professor who bought me a couple of wonderful dinners?"

I told her I was the one and then asked if I could speak to Mr. Mainwaring on the phone.

"Sure you can. Oh, by the way, do I get another free dinner for this permission?" she asked. After I assured her she did, she put the call through.

When John answered I identified myself and said, "Do you think you can find the time this evening about seven o'clock to be at our house in Edisto for dinner? (I gave him our Palmetto Boulevard address.) By the way, after dinner you might like to take your now brown-haired wife off our hands. By tonight she might be a brunette again if she manages to get to a drug store or beauty parlor."

John (trying to hide his excitement, I guess) said he thought he could be there by seven o'clock and take care of this onerous task.

Chapter Twenty-Three

Back to the Scene of the Crime

T wo days before we were to leave Edisto and return home, a brunch was given in our honor at the First Universe Bank in Charleston. The invited guests included Bobbie Mainwaring with her hair black again; her husband, John; Lt. Seabrook; Captain La Roche; the Manigaults along with all the persons who worked in the bank. In addition, the mayor of Charleston, William Tradd, was present.

George Mengedoht, who had just been officially promoted to the job of bank president, conducted the affair. There was certainly a festive atmosphere among the bank employees and the police. The air of suspicion that had existed the last few weeks for all the bank people was gone. They felt like they were starting a new life. I think they had wondered all this time whether one or more of their associates had been guilty of stealing the money. After the guests had finished eating, Mr. Mengedoht gave a little talk expressing his gratitude to Fiona and me for solving the second robbery and the sand castle murder at Edisto.

Sometimes Fiona can be a little cynical. She was exactly that this morning as she whispered in my ear, "Mr. Mengedoht should be grateful to us. We not only solved the mysteries, but we also recovered a large proportion of the bank's money. Furthermore, our work resulted in his being promoted to the job of bank president."

Both Captain La Roche and Lt. Seabrook said to us, "You did it even though it was beginning to look as though the mysteries would never be solved."

Captain La Roche then added, "From my viewpoint there is another great thing involved in your solving this case. Maybe it will shut up that *Post and Courier* editorialist Guignard for a little while. He is always jumping on us when we have trouble solving a crime."

They both said they would be delighted to have us work with them in the future on other puzzling cases they encountered. These statements made me shudder a little, while they made Fiona smile from head to toe. She again whispered to me saying, "How about right now?"

It seems the insurance group had earlier announced they would provide a substantial financial reward for anyone who provided information leading to the solution of the mysteries. Mr. Mengedoht said the reward money would be turned over to Fiona and me. At the end of his little speech Fiona asked if she could say a word or two. Upon being given permission, she thanked the president for his kind words but then said a large percentage of the credit should be given to Bobbie Mainwaring. It was her recall of events in the bank that enabled Fiona to solve the mysteries. As a result, the reward money was split into three equal parts. One part would go to Bobbie, and the other two parts would go to Fiona and me. After receiving my check and seeing how large it was, I wondered if I had previously told you how much I love these old, exquisite, beautiful, lovely, gorgeous wooden tennis racquets that are to be hung on our den walls.

Fiona said she was delighted with her share of the money and couldn't wait to return to those lovely antique stores over on King Street to pick up a few items she had liked. I confess I said I would go back to the antique store, also on King Street, that had all those old golf tees and other golf items and spend some of my money. Fiona and I jokingly asked if we could cash our reward checks at another bank as we didn't want to receive any of the stolen bills and have Captain La Roche come after us.

Mr. Mengedoht went on to say all the wooden tennis racquets would be forwarded to Fiona when the police and the district attorney released them, probably after a period of at least several months. I think the bank employees were glad to see the last of the racquets because they probably reminded them of the robberies and murder that had occurred at their work place and the concerns and suspicions they must have had at times concerning their fellow employees. Was one of them a killer and thief? I also had the feeling the senior bank officials didn't want them around either as they would remind them of the robbery. They probably didn't want someone else to start hiding money in the tennis racquet handles.

As the swan neck golf club did not figure in the robbery, Mr. Mengedoht, much to my delight, presented the beautiful club to me. I thought I oohed and aahed over the club about the right amount, but when I looked over at Fiona, she looked a little disgusted.

Just before this delightful brunch was over Mayor Tradd presented us with a key to the Holy City. He came over to us when the meeting was officially over and asked us to tell him of the places we had visited in Charleston. After we did this he proceeded to take us on a several hour personally guided tour of some other attractions in the city. He first took us on a helicopter ride over the city. Then back on the ground he took us to see the Hunley submarine, the great cable-stayed Arthur Ravenel, Jr. Bridge over the Cooper River Next there was a boat excursion to Morris Island and finally a tour of James Island. This latter area was of particular interest to me because my great great great grandfather enlisted in the Confederate Army there in 1862 at the age of seventeen. (Despite this fact, I still can't get into the St. Cecilia Society.)

After this delightful tour with the mayor, he dropped us off at our car parked at the bank. Though it was now rather late in the afternoon, we drove once again through several of the beautiful streets of the historic district. As we looked at the lovely homes, Fiona said she was almost ready to move here to live. I thought her interest in the area was primarily architectural but then she said rather wistfully, "It is great to have solved this mystery. But sometimes I think I'm happier not when an investigation is over, but when we are in the middle of a case eagerly following some clue and happily anticipating a solution. As they say when it's over, it's over."

She continued, "I wonder if I could move my architecture office here and have any success obtaining clients. Perhaps The Citadel would take you on as a civil engineering instructor."

I shook my head. "They know me too well. I doubt they would give me a moment's consideration."

By this time I realized she was thinking of moving to the Holy City not because of its beauty, historic interest, and the nearby beaches, but because she thought there would be more crimes to try to tackle here. My thoughts were certainly verified when she said, "I understand the crime rate is somewhat high in Charleston. If we lived here Captain La Roche might let us work on various murder and robbery cases."

She further showed what her interests really were when we drove past another bank and with her eyes sparkling she exclaimed, "Maybe they will have a robbery and a murder or two at this bank. We may be called on to help solve the case. Wouldn't that be wonderful?"

Fiona is a native of Vermont, a state that seems so green, beautiful, peaceful, and free from litter and mayhem, and yet she seems to want the terrain where she is located to be littered with corpses. How could that state with its beauty and tranquility have raised this almost blood thirsty wife of mine? As we drove back to Edisto, I had the feeling she was dreaming of various crimes, while my dreams pertained to swimming, sunbathing, and lounging on the beach with her.

We both hoped to come back to Edisto and Charleston in the near future. There are so many things in and around the Holy City to see other than the ones we had seen on this trip. For instance, there is the Charleston Tea Plantation, the Gibbes Museum of Art, the water taxi dolphin cruise and a pub tour (I would like this one, but I'm not so sure about Fiona unless some violent crime had occurred in one of them). In addition there are the nearby beaches and a Late Great Unpleasantness walking tour. On second thought we better not do this walking tour together. She has decidedly different views from me on the subject. Such a walk together might be dangerous for me. It would rather be like my playing mixed doubles in tennis

THE SKETCHING DETECTIVE AND THE SECRET ROBBERY

with her as my partner. She might use my head to change her racquet into a warped jeu de paume one.

I understand a few weeks later Mr. Rivers made a formal confession to the effect that he had carried out the second robbery and had killed Martha Ulmer on the beach at Edisto. He said he had planned this robbery several years in advance. His thought was if an armed robbery of his bank ever occurred, he would be ready to implement his plan for an immediate second robbery. He said, if successful, the money he obtained in this manner would not be reduced by taxation. He had always wanted to retire to the Caribbean and was just trying to build up his retirement funds so that day would be nearer.

Another difficult investigation had come to a close. Maybe Fiona should consider giving up architecture to pursue private investigating full time. Whatever she does, I'm sticking with engineering.

Printed in the United States
By Bookmasters